Tales of the Scorpion

an anthology of stories and poems
by Northants Writers' Ink

edited and introduced by
Michael J Richards
Chair, Northants Writers' Ink

CONTENTS

Introduction

by Michael J Richards

The tale with a twist has a surprise ending which, on reflection, should not have been a surprise. The writer has led the reader believe he is going in one direction but both end up somewhere else.

The ending is consistent with how the story has gone. Everything that has happened arises naturally from the action but it is the reader, not the writer, who leads himself astray. He has not read the map correctly.

There are two types of tale with a twist.

The first is the story clothed in language capable of credible ambiguity whose interpretation, like the picture that is either two faces or a wine-glass, depends on how you view the world. The ending follows the interpretation you didn't follow, didn't know it was there to follow. You are so surprised and delighted that you go back and re-read the story with the other interpretation in your head, now seeing the well-laid clues, admiring the writer's dexterity.

Seven of the thirteen stories in this anthology fit that description.

Other tales with twists are those that take an unexpected turn without using ambivalent language. The reader drives along a straight road when, suddenly, the writer takes a sharp left. The new territory is in keeping with the terrain so far travelled but now starkly different. Sometimes called "the surprise ending", it shocks the reader without leaving them feeling betrayed.

Six of the stories in this anthology follow that road.

* * * * *

Roald Dahl is known for exceeding expectation in this genre, "Lamb to the Slaughter" being probably one of the most well known examples. But I cannot recommend highly enough "Triangle" by the American novelist Jeffery Deaver. It has everything a tale with a twist should have. It is master story telling at its best.

Other writers have used the novel and delivered twists. One thinks of *A Tale of Two Cities* (1859), by Charles Dickens; *The Hound of the Baskervilles* (1902), Arthur Conan Doyle; *Rebecca* (1938), Daphne du Maurier; *The Third Man* (1950), Graham Greene; *Fight Club*, Chuck Palahniuk (1996); *Harry Potter and the Philosopher's Stone* (1997), J K Rowling; *Gone Girl* (2012), Gillian Flynn.

And one should never underestimate Agatha Christie who, while having a reputation for writing whodunits in poorly styled prose, excelled in the art of twist tales containing the qualities outlined in the opening paragraphs of this introduction.

The short story "Triangle at Rhodes" and the novels *And Then There were None* and *A Murder is Announced* stand out as being fine contributions. *The Murder of Roger Ackroyd*, of course, is one of the greatest of all in this genre.

And finally – oddly – Oscar Wilde. *The Importance of Being Earnest* must be not only one of the great works in the English language, but also one of the prime examples of twist tales. One is left dizzy by its magickry.

* * * * *

Tales of the Scorpion is a collection of writings, all of which have a twist – or sting – in their tales.

Written by members of Northants Writers' Ink, it marks the group's first publishing venture.

Formed in October 2013, Northants Writers' Ink is a writers' group based in Wellingborough, Northamptonshire, England.

New members can find more information and how to join at www.northantswritersink.net, by emailing northantswritersink@outlook.com or by going to www.meetup.com.

* * * * *

Guido's Door, by **Allan J Shipham**, opens our anthology. It is an enigmatic tale of murder, imprisonment, thoughtful police officers and phantasmal mystery, written in a style evocative in places of Joseph Conrad. It is great fun and made me read on, always wanting more. This is Allan's first published piece of fiction.

Helen Aird offers two tales. *Today I Saved a Life* is a short piece which opens in black, Blue Peter-ish "Here's one I made earlier" mode before taking a sharp left turn. Helen's other contribution, *The Queen of Swords*, set in the world of tarot, is an amusing tale of love, gossip and lack of self-awareness. It is worth reading more than once to get its full measure and – true to form – knowing the ending enhances the experience.

Deborah's Diary, by **Jason McClean**, takes the reader into a different world altogether. Here we have a pleasant young lady, Deborah, with a secret hobby, which she delights in documenting in every detail. It is a sober narrative, made even more chilling for its lack of overblown, dramatic emotion – and a sting that leaves you wondering what was really going on.

Kim Grove presents four pieces. *The Empty House* is a very short, delightful piece, which will bring a smile. Equally, *Tram: San Francisco* does not take itself too seriously, either – and all the better for it. *A Different Type of Service* plays on the theme of identity, which Kim takes further in *Secrets and Lies*. This story has quite a few twists and turns before reaching its natural, though bizarre, conclusion.

We then move into poetry. **Liz Heywood** gives us a selection of reflective poems, each in one way or another grappling with the theme of loss, each with its own twist but in miniature. For me, *From Second Wife* stands out among the *embarras de richesse*. Then Liz shows another side with *Making an English Lady*, a story of lust, sexual awakening and joyously unapologetic descriptions of human physical and emotional interaction. Irresistible.

Michael J Richards offers *Where do we go from here?* a tale of two lovers lazing in the afternoon sun. *Lost in a Fog* shows a desperate mother trying to get her son to his annual check-up. *Learnin' the family business* inhabits the gangster world in New York, 1926. Northants Writers' Ink's first anthology concludes with two men trekking the Brecon Beacons, one teaching the other how to read a map.

Which where we came in.

Michael J Richards
Wellingborough, Northamptonshire
August 2015

Allan J Shipham

Allan J Shipham lives in Wellingborough with his children, but was born in London and grew up in Leeds. He has worked as a college tutor, stock market trader, management consultant and within the construction industry. He has volunteered with various charities and supported people with challenging and unfortunate backgrounds.

As an author, Allan has had newsletter articles and a couple of poems printed, but this is his first published story. Allan became a writer quite late in life, and enjoys being a member of Northants Writers' Ink (he is the group's treasurer), developing his skills and networking.

Allan has several projects in the pipeline and hopes to publish more stories and novels in the future.

Guido's Door

by Allan Shipham

The only sound through the darkness was the clink of the master keys and the muffled whimper of a penitent man. The night-guard made his way diligently checking the doors and performing his regular welfare checks.

Saltmarsh Prison was never considered a model of modern penal reform by anyone who visited, anyone imprisoned or anyone who worked there. It was, however, an excellent place to store away some of society's worst offenders, until such time that they were considered reformed and fit to return to society. As the lone guard, Garney, walked his wing, he glanced around the Victorian brickwork and architraves. He wondered what it had looked like when it was new. He paused at the entrance staircase to admire the stained-glass window. There was a patch where the stained glass had been replaced with clear glass after a prisoner smashed it during a riot. The guard's concentration was disturbed by muffled screech from one of the cells. He looked along the balcony.

Garney peered tentatively into each of the cells, along what had become known as suicide balcony. Each prisoner had their own reason for being there and therefore a reason to be subject to hourly welfare checks. Mistakes had been made in the past and the Governor was determined they wouldn't be repeated.

Garney checked the name slate alongside the next room he was going to check. Adrian Spencer. Adrian, or Fingers Spencer, as he was known, was a small-time art burglar. He'd lost two of his fingers climbing over a razor wire wall, hence his nickname. He kept himself to himself. Most of the prisoners' cells on this balcony were lit by dull night lights. As the guard peered into a single spyglass with his right eye, his iris widened adjusting to the light. As he scanned across the cell, his face drew closer to the door and then pulled away in horror at what he saw. He looked up and down the corridor, then slammed his fist on the emergency alert button. Protocol dictated that he wait until help arrived, but he grabbed at his key cluster and picked out the key for the door, and pushed it into the lock. A clunk echoed through the halls as he turned the key, the door opened.

When his colleague arrived from the control room, he froze to the spot as he started to enter. Before him, his workmate was kneeling beside the ravaged body of a skinny, tattooed middle-aged man. The dead man had scratches across his face and arms, where he'd been in a struggle, there was blood splattered all over the bed from his neck and a puddle of blood on the floor.

"What happened?"

"I've no idea! I was doing my rounds and... I found this."

"This is the second one now!" the guard said.

The Governor arrived within an hour. From his expression, he didn't like being woken, but when he saw the scene he realised he needed to be there. By this time, four prison guards were standing close by on the balcony, and two policemen were asking questions and making notes.

"Was he in his cell?"

"Yes, sir," responded a guard, stepping aside to let the Governor appraise the situation.

"What are they doing here?" He pointed in the direction of the police.

"They were visiting Beasley on A wing, sir." He glanced at his colleague. "I think there was a death in the family."

"How can this happen?" the warden asked, glancing back at the cell. "Twice in the same prison, on the same balcony, of the same wing... Two murders under our noses!" The Governor looked for one of his night guards, Garney. He was being questioned by one of the police guards, both were leaning on the spiral staircase at the end of the balcony.

"Garney, what happened here?"

"Sir, there is no way he did it himself, and there was no-one in his cell. Check the cameras!" He shook his head in disbelief. "I have no idea."

The Governor looked up to the balcony camera, a red pulse led light confirming they were live and still recording.

"I want to see those tapes!" He looked again at Garney. "Are you okay?"

"I'll be alright, sir. I'm just a bit shaken... you know," he replied.

"Yes... of course."

One of the police officers stepped forward.

"DC William Bedford," stated the officer, introducing himself.

"Detective Constable," responded the Governor. "At this unearthly hour?"

"We were already on site sir, visiting one of the other wings."

8

The governor nodded. "How can I help?"

"We'll need to see the tapes to see if they corroborate your Guard's testimony."

"I agree. We can do that straight away. I'll take you to the control room."

As they made their way, Bedford explained that he'd called in forensics and a photographer to take pictures. They examined the tapes and confirmed that no-one had entered the cell since lock-up, and no-one had been close to it since the last checks. None of the prison guards had blood on their hands or clothes at any time. There were no bloody footprints or any signs or entry or exit.

The crime scene investigators quietly and swiftly processed the scene, and removed the body for post mortem examination. By the time the other prisoners were awake, the investigators had left the building and the police would return later in the day to interrogate the other prisoners on the wing. As everyone was locked down, there didn't seem to be any good reason to disturb the morning routines. As daylight broke and shone through the grilled windows, the prison guards could hear some of the prisoners stirring. They looked at each other and shook their heads. Prison life was a tough job, but they knew when there was a murder, they were in for a difficult day.

* * * * *

Several days went past. The prisoners were angry when they found out about another unexplained murder inside the prison. Each of them feared for themselves, as the murders had no pattern or apparent motive. There was a lot of unrest, and it was hard to get the prisoners to settle down after lights out. What puzzled the staff was how the victims had been murdered while locked in their own cells.

At first, the prisoners suspected that a prison guard had done it. Neither guard who discovered the deaths had any issues with the victims, and neither would've been able to enter the cells or attack the victims without being heard. When word got around about Garney finding the second corpse, some of the prisoners were sympathetic, and even offered him words of support. There was also a range of theories about the ghost of another prisoner coming back from the dead to claim his revenge on the inmates. Another crazy suggestion was an invisible man who walked into the prisoner's room with them at night, murdered them, then calmly walked out past the prison guard when they entered the cell the next day. The truth was, until it was resolved, hardly anyone had a good night's sleep at Saltmarsh.

The prisoners inevitably started to suspect each other. An artist called Guido who freaked out the other inmates with his general behaviour soon became a suspect. He had been sent down for attempted murder, but he'd been seen biting the heads off rats and painting his face with squashed cockroaches. His cell wasn't next to the victims, but that didn't stop the rumours. They even suspected a defrocked priest. Someone suggested he'd done a deal with the devil after he murdered a parishioner to get at her life savings. Despite all the ideas and fights that started, no-one really knew what happened and the only person likely to find out was the murderer's next victim.

* * * * *

Darkness descended quickly the next evening. The storm that brewed outside took away its share of the light. Prison Guard John French was in charge of the patrols. The atmosphere at the prison was tense, the thunder and lightening outside disturbed the smooth running of the prison. French paused and listened at each cell door. At one, he craned across to hear the fearful inmate saying a prayer, blessing himself and weeping. Even the prison guards were unnerved. Whatever had murdered the prisoners would be able to walk through the doors and walls, and go anywhere it wanted. It hadn't struck a guard yet, but one of them could be the next victim. The guard in the control room monitored French as he moved around the building.

French methodically peered into each cell. Eventually he came to the penultimate one. Prisoner David Duke's name and number were scrawled on a white board next to his door. Duke was a small-time crook. He'd fallen out with his gang after a failed building society job several years before. He wasn't in prison for the attempted robbery or for falling out with members of his gang. David was found guilty of murdering a couple of gang mates with bleach and weed killer, after they blamed him when it all went wrong. Luckily, two of them got to hospital in time and the doctors were able to heal them leaving only facial scars. The other two were not so lucky. Both died of chemical burns to the mouth and throat. French could see the prisoner was asleep on his bunk. Most cells hosted two prisoners, but in this area of the prison, the cells were smaller and suited only one. Domestos Dave, as he'd become known, had got it into his head that one of his victims had returned as the ghost. His mental health had been in question.

French's boots slowly paced away, and silence returned. David stirred in his sleep, his nose twitched and he mumbled something incoherent. He was asleep, but his sleep was far from peaceful. The wall between his cell and the one next to him trembled and then started to shudder. Someone was forcing the wall from the opposite side. The thud of the shunt was enough to be heard, but not enough to wake him. Another thud, this time slightly louder, followed by a sprinkle as dust and debris fell to the ground close to the wall. David continued to sleep. On the third thud, a shape about the size of a door, started to stand proud from the wall, respecting the pattern of the existing Victorian bricks. By the fourth thud, the doorway protruded into the cell. Someone was on the other side trying to get through. David stirred in his sleep, the brick dust was teasing his nose, he sneezed, woke briefly, glanced around his cell dazed, and returned back to his sleep.

A single hand emerged from the dark, and its fingers wrapped themselves around the door. The hand was wrapped in bandages soiled with blood and paint. The blood was dry and dark. The hand tensed up and the new door quietly swung open further.

David moved around in his slumber trying to find a more comfortable position. As he relaxed, the bandaged hand slowly moved effortlessly through the air toward his head. As it got close to his face, it moved down to his neck, finding a suitable place, and hung in the air. David breathed in and as he breathed out the hand grabbed his throat and squeezed very tightly. David woke with a start, unable to breathe in or out. He tried to sit upright and grabbed at his own throat. Half-sitting up, and as he struggled to gasp, his eyes met those of the man who'd got into his cell. David realised what was happening. He reached toward his attacker with his free hand, but he was weak and couldn't grab him. His other hand gave way and he fell back on to his bed again. David used his hand to grab the arm around his throat. He squeezed it with all the might and force he could muster. It wasn't enough, the assailant was very strong, overpowering and skilled at what he was doing.

Aware David was weakening, the attacker drew closer to him and pressed his weight on to David's chest, squeezing his throat harder. The attacker drew a fork from his pocket. The edge of a metal fork had been sharpened into a blade. He sliced into David's throat. Blood started to pump out. David let out a frustrated growl, realising he was losing the struggle. His eyes bulged, his cheeks reddened, and his lips, nose and ears went blue. Suddenly, he went limp and his eyes glazed over. His murderer maintained his grip for a minute longer, ensuring he'd finished off his prize. Then he rolled him over to mask the wound should the night guard return for his next welfare check.

David's murderer stood up and massaged the wrist he'd used to strangle him. He could see the blood leaking from his throat had stopped its regular pulsing, and was now just oozing slowly into the bed sheets. He went back to the portal and through the wall. The door moved back towards the wall and shuffled back into its original position until there was no join. The only indication that something had happened was a small trace of plaster and brick dust on the floor near where the door had been. For all the security, guards and locks, David was dead.

* * * * *

French put his coffee cup down and picked up his keys.

"Best head out."

The controller looked up at the clock,

"Has it been an hour since the last patrol?"

"Yes, job's gotta be done!" French smiled. He liked his job, even if some elements that were distressing or repetitive.

The controller glanced at the wall of CCTV screens.

"Looks quiet out there tonight," he said, ticking a box on a check schedule.

"Yes, that's what worries me." French looked over at the screens and then at the control room door. He left and made his way to the welfare balcony.

When French approached Duke's cell, he paused in his tracks and the hair on his neck and arms stood on end. It was strangely cooler than everywhere else. He first looked back down where he'd come from and then along the corridor where the cells were. There was no-one else around. He stared up at the wing CCTV. The power light was on. It gave him some peace of mind that his controller was watching him. He peered into David's cell, the prisoner appeared to be asleep, but facing away from the door. French took one more look before moving away.

French had an instinct that something didn't seem right. David's chest wasn't rising or sinking, and he noticed a shimmering puddle he hadn't noticed before underneath the bed. Against all his training, he froze. It seemed like minutes, but it was only seconds, he drew a breath and then his training kicked in.

He looked for and then reached across to the alarm

button, and pressed it firmly. The silent alarm activated again, red lights flashed on and off in the control room.

His controller arrived. French already had his master key in the lock. He turned the key and they both entered.

"Duke! Wake Up!" shouted French.

There was no response.

"Wake up Duke!" the controller shouted.

They looked at each other. French indicated that he was going closer. His controller readied his baton.

French shook Duke at arm's length. David's limp body fell back on to his pillow, his face staring toward the ceiling.

French placed two fingers into David's neck.

"No pulse," he shouted and shifted position kneeling side on, so he could start chest compressions.

His colleague pointed to the slash in David's neck.

"You're wasting your time. He's dead, John."

French slumped back.

"I can't believe it," French despaired. "How the hell can this happen?" He looked down at his hands, covered in blood. "I don't understand."

The controller turned on the tap in the corner sink. "Here, wash your hands," he said. "Rinse the sink after, they'll be looking for forensics."

French washed his hands, and moved toward the wall where the door had been. As he got to the wall, he stooped to the floor. "Look at this!" His interest was drawn to a small trace of dust on the floor. He pressed his finger into the dust and stood up.

"Charlie, look at this."

"What's that, John?"

"I found this dust by the wall."

"Don't touch anything else," he said. "Come out, I'll call the Governor, and we'll show the police. This is the first real clue anyone's found."

They walked out of the cell and the controller locked the door.

The closest prisoners were disturbed by the noise and woke up, they asked questions and made noises through their locked doors, their catcalls disturbing others further down the corridor.

"What's happening?"

"Has someone else been slashed in their sleep?"

"Who's got rubbed out this time?"

"Hey, Walt, did the ghost kill you?"

"No, man, it wasn't me."

"Frenchie, did you kill someone?"

"Hey! What's happening?"

When the police arrived, their presence caused a new frenzy among the prisoners, scowling, spitting and banging of metal plates against the food service hatches. They couldn't see what was happening but they could hear voices.

"DC Bedford."

"Yes, you attended last time," the Governor acknowledged.

Bedford shook his head.

"Who's the victim?"

"David Dukes, a nobody!"

The Governor introduced the controller to DC Bedford.

"One of my guards noticed something unusual this time. I'm not sure if it's relevant," said the controller, unlocking the door.

"I'm open to any ideas at the moment," said the detective, as he walked into the cell.

"Ah, someone's washed their hands in the sink,

this is new!" announced Bedford.

"Ah no, not that. That was one of my officers after he tried to revive him." The controller pointed to the dust. "The floors were mopped yesterday afternoon," he stated. "We can't think of any reason why the floor here should be dusty."

"Most strange."

There was a lot of dust but it was finely sprinkled.

Bedford pressed his finger into a few fragments of the dust, he smelled it and inspected it closely to see if it was powder or crystals. "I'll get forensics to take a look at some of this." He stood up and looked closely at the wall. "Maybe there's a secret entrance to a corridor, or another room?"

"A secret corridor?"

"Yes, these old Victorian buildings are notorious for that kind of thing."

"Rubbish, I've worked here for years!" The controller stepped back, and took another look at the wall. "No! There's another cell directly next to this one."

"Maybe it wasn't this wall." Bedford ran his fingers over the wall looking for an irregularity. "I'll get this crime scene checked out with a fine tooth comb."

"There's no way anyone came through that wall from the cell next door," said French, who'd followed them in.

"Why?" asked Bedford.

"Because that is Harry the Hammer's cell, he was murdered in there last month. The Ghost's first victim. We ain't put anyone else in there since."

"The Ghost?"

"That's what they're calling him, the murderer!"

The police eliminated all possibility of secret corridors or passages. Everyone checked and rechecked their statements and CCTV footage. Time passed. There were no more murders and things returned to what was considered normal at the prison. The investigation became less of a priority to the police, questions were asked, but no-one had any answers. Several inmates were discharged and new ones received. All of the rooms where the murders took place were abandoned and the suicide balcony was moved over to the next wing.

No-one ever admitted to the murders. Rumours continued. Some said aliens did it. Some thought they killed themselves. There was even a suggestion that one of the prisoners, a painter called Guido, could walk through walls. But there were no actual witnesses to anything.

The case remained unresolved and the documents were filed away until there were any new developments.

* * * * *

Maurice De Fethney was a jewellery thief. Several months after his release, while robbing a jeweller, he was arrested again. DCI James McCallum and arresting officer DC Rose Mead asked questions. DC William Bedford sat in on the questioning. He'd recognised Maurice in the custody suite. Mead stepped out to check some information and Bedford asked if he could ask a couple of questions.

"So, tell me again what you heard while you were at Saltmarsh. Time's past now, you don't have to keep any secrets."

"I told ya, I ain't sayin' nothin'."

DC Bedford leaned toward the twitching ex-con.

The man was nervous and uncomfortable.

Bedford removed his glasses, folded them and placed them on the table between them.

"Okay, please... tell me everything you heard or knew about this Guido character."

DCI McCallum nodded in agreement, and looked Maurice in the eye.

"Them things ain't for sharin', see," Maurice retorted. The middle-aged, shabby man looked at the officers. "Ain't nothin' in it all, anyway." He shook his head several times, and shifted his stare to the table.

"We already know what you said in your statement at the time, I just want you to repeat it back to us, so we can see if we missed anything," Bedford stated.

"This isn't about this jewellery theft, this is a different investigation. If you have any new information, you'd be simply helping me with my enquiries."

"What's in it for me, then?"

"Well, if we cut a deal with you, it'll look like we're doing you a favour," McCallum explained. "Let's be clear, I'm not here for any favours."

"Why should I tell you anything?" Maurice stared at Bedford.

"You'd be helping us to solve some murders. Now, that could reflect positively on your sentence, should you be sent down for the jewellery... the jewellery that got you arrested today."

Maurice made a scraping noise as he pushed his chair away from the table. He crossed his arms in protest.

"I ain't done nothin', and you know it!" he shouted.

D C Mead knocked twice and came back into the room clutching three mugs of tea and a plastic wallet.

"The fingerprints match, they'll throw the book at you after last time."

Maurice noticed the results wallet Mead placed on the table. He could see technology had caught him again. He shook his head and rubbed a prison tattoo on the back of his hand, then mumbled to himself.

Bedford got up, took a mug of tea, and let Mead take her seat.

"What about the deal?" Maurice asked, anxious that Bedford was about to leave.

Mead glanced at the other two officers.

"There's no deal. we asked if you were prepared to help us with our enquiries," stated Bedford.

"Yeah, but you said it would help..."

"I said it might reflect positively on any sentencing."

Maurice mopped his brow and shook his head in frustration. After some thought, he spoke. "Okay, I'll tell you what I heard, but I want it on record that I was helpful, see. Makes no difference to me now!"

McCallum and Mead took a statement about the jewellery theft. Bedford set the recorder to take a statement on the Saltmarsh murders. He also got out his notepad and pen. He liked to jot key points down.

"While I was at Saltmarsh, I was on the same floor as them there murders." Maurice looked at all three officers who were now listening intensely. "Well, after the third, we was all gathered in the R and R." Maurice stopped talking so Bedford could catch up writing notes. "That's the rest and relaxation room," he said.

"I know what R and R means."

"We called it rough and ready," he smiled, but the others were not interested. "Well, there was this painter, see, and he had a way of keepin' out of everyone's business 'n' all. He was no trouble." Maurice motioned to the cup of tea that McCallum was finishing off.

"In a minute..."

"Well, see, this painter got picked on, 'cos' he wasn't siding with any of the gangs. He was trying to stay out of all of that." Maurice hesitated.

The officers glanced at each other.

"Well, what I knows is, the guy in the next cell to 'is, picks a fight he does. He was moaning 'bout him snoring or something. Well, that night, he was number three. That's all I'm saying."

Bedford looked frantically through his notes, turning pages, he speedread a couple of passages. "So you're saying you witnessed an argument between David Dukes and the painter the day Dukes died?"

"Yeah, Domestos Dave, the poisoner, that's 'im."

"Would that be Guido?" Bedford asked, looking for confirmation. "The painter?"

Maurice looked at Mead, he nodded, but didn't speak.

"For the benefit of the tape... "

"Yeah, Guido and Domestos Dave had an argument."

"Who was this painter? This Guido?" asked McCallum.

"Dunno, never spoke with 'im. But, it was then that we started to fink he was the one who done the others in."

Bedford scrawled as much as he could in his best shorthand.

"Why wasn't anything said at the time?"

"We did, but you know the screws, they ain't interested. And the pigs, we think they thought the screws did it... Begging your pardon."

Bedford dismissed the 'pig' insult as he scribbled down notes.

"Why wasn't this Guido arrested if there was a murder, and he was the main suspect in the next cell?" Mead was unfamiliar with the case. Maurice shuffled his chair closer to the table.

"Well, that's where it gets creepy, see. They was all done in as they slept."

"Then it must have been the cellmates. The doors would've been locked."

"The doors were all locked down." Maurice nodded. "See, in that part of the nick, the old part, some of the cells are one man only. They don't use them now, 'cept for storage. They put all the suicides in the new wing."

"So, a lone prisoner, in a single cell, is murdered and no-one went anywhere near?" quizzed Mead.

"Yes!" replied Bedford, already familiar with the details.

"That's impossible. It must be a secret passage or something, I thought they'd shut all the dodgy prisons." Mead was sharp and to the point even if she was a little green.

"There were no secret passages. I saw the cell myself," Maurice responded.

"And I checked it, every inch of it," added Bedford.

Maurice lowered his voice. The atmosphere became more sinister. "Some say it was the Ghost!"

Mead and McCallum drew back into the chairs, slightly startled by the statement.

"Well, I don't believe in them ghosties and

ghoulies I tell you," asserted Maurice. "But, I'll tell ya, there's no way in, no way out. They was dead. Strangled in their sleep, all of 'em."

"It must have been a prison guard, it's the only way." Mead rationalised. "Who had keys? Who was monitoring the CCTV?"

"I checked all of that out!" Bedford confirmed.

"And another thing," interrupted Maurice. "Them doors made a right clatter as they rattled open and close. Different cells and never a witness I tell ya!" "It weren't no 'uman what did it'"

They thanked Maurice for his story. He'd contributed a little, but Bedford still didn't have anything he could investigate.

Maurice was taken away to be booked into the cells overnight.

McCallum noticed Bedford's note pad as he packed it away. Not only were there written notes, Bedford had sketched images of the cell, some of the prisoners, cars, buildings and maps.

"Good drawings!" McCallum commented.

"Yes, they help me to explain things, remember crime scenes and it inspires ideas."

"Quite a skill, no doubt in that."

"Yeah, when I did art at Whittlebury Art College I never suspected I'd be able to use my skills in any job. I thought it was just a doss."

They both moved to the staff canteen to talk some more about the case. There was fresh air from the windows and more space to move about and lay out evidence. Holding the door open, Bedford momentarily placed his documents and glasses case on the counter. He didn't notice the glasses case roll off, and drop on the floor behind it.

* * * * *

"Tell me more about this painter, Guido." McCallum asked Bedford as they left the building.

"The psychiatric report detailed that he preferred his own company and tried not to mix with the other inmates. He was doing time because he was caught fiddling the books at his business, a specialist Dark Arts shop in Camden."

"Dark Arts?"

"Yeah, you know, voodoo and witchcraft. The reports suggest he was harmless enough, apart from creeping out anyone who tried to work with him. His neighbour was pushed down some stairs after an altercation. Guido was sent down for a stretch, but he won on appeal and the case was thrown out."

Bedford scanned his notes in the notepad he'd used at the time. He didn't usually carry them all around but he'd picked that one up when he went to the custody suite to interview Maurice. "Damn, I can't find my glasses. While he was there, I think he took up an art therapy rehabilitation session, but his work was assessed to be obscure and not very creative."

"Like what?"

"Parts of ugly faces, dead beetles, petrified trees, oh, and a painted door."

"A door?" McCallum repeated.

"No! A painted door."

"A painted door?" McCallum repeated what was said. By putting great emphasis on the words, he seemed to think this was more important than Bedford did.

"Yes, a painted door. There was a statement from one of the prison guards... er... Garney. He overheard three prisoners talking about the door painting being how Guido was able to go through walls. Rumour was he used the painting and his black magic to walk through the walls. I haven't seen it, but by all accounts it was just a close up picture of a brightly painted door on an old farm or a cottage. It seems the painting itself was dull, but it was the only piece he took back to his cell from the art room."

"You ought to pay him a visit, and ask some questions. Where's he serving?"

"He's not!"

"Dead?"

"No, he was released at the appeal. They thought the neighbour staged the fall."

"How come he was released, if he was a suspect in these murders?"

"No evidence. All they ever found was a pile of dust." Bedford shrugged his shoulders. "The prisoners on that wing said they didn't hear anything the night Domestos Dave was killed. If you can believe a prisoner."

McCallum sipped his coffee.

"Here's the funny thing, chief," Bedford said. "When they released Guido, apart from his keys and some change, the door picture was the only thing he took with him."

"All hocus-pocus by the look of things," McCallum concluded. "Nothing you've told me or we've discussed has any credibility. I'm not sure how any of it helps your investigation," he sighed.

Bedford gathered his notes and slid them into his briefcase.

"I'm sure there's something I'm missing. The DCI is keen to see this put to bed, but with no suspects, no access and no witnesses, I'm gonna find this one hard to close. In some ways, I feel I am close. In others, I feel it's never going to be solved. I have to go, I have to make an urgent call."

He left the reception area and made his way to the car park. He paused and made a mobile call.

* * * * *

In an artist's studio, a dishevelled character gathered fuel carriers and fabric and stacked them beside a canvas that leaned against an easel. The painting appeared to be unfinished or painted in haste, as the paint didn't reach all the edges and around the edge there appeared to be burnt ash marks. His dark oversized smock followed him around the room like a shadow. Streaks of light from a skylight lit his face as he moved around. He paused and used a finger to count the items before him as he took stock. Then he moved across the room to a table and picked up a file. It looked official and had a worn ink-stamp on the front. As he opened the file, the light from outside reflected off a photograph and several documents. He shuffled through the documents and re-read a handwritten page. He glanced at his watch, folded and replaced the file.

A bronze ceremonial burner stood on a bronze tripod in the corner of the room. Inside the bowl were several large branch twigs already half-burnt to embers. Black smoke rose straight up and lightly filled the ceiling space. It then dissolved out of a small high window. It wasn't enough to cause any alarm, but could have frustrated any neighbours.

The suspicious character reached for a couple of bottles from a shelf. He opened two of the bottles and stood them on a table near the burner. He then opened a shoebox and took out some items. He looked at his watch again and began to chant in an ancient language. During the chant, he threw the shoebox items into the bowl and sprinkled some of the bottle contents over the embers. As he spoke, flames changed from yellow to green, then to blue. A purple flame raged from the bowl illuminating the whole room and the street outside. The artist then took one of the twigs and stirred the contents around the bowl. He removed a twig and rubbed it around the canvas that leaned on the easel. Sparkles emerged from the canvas and the image shimmered. The artist replaced the twig and continued his chant. He wrapped a bloody bandage around his hands.

The painting of a door's frame transformed into the shape of large construction blocks before the artist's eyes and he then pushed the brickwork with his full strength without knocking over the canvas or the easel.

* * * * *

Luke worked as a night patrol officer at New Meadows Shopping Centre. In the basement, access corridors were lined with power cables and heater boiler pipes everywhere, stock cages and waste bins lined the passages. Background noise filled the air as the water and gas were pumped through the pipes to keep the building warm. Luke had performed his checks. He wasn't expecting any problems.

In an isolated passage, there was a thud and one of the breezeblock walls started to move. Dust and debris started to peel away from the wall as the second thud opened up a doorway. Again, a bandaged hand emerged from the void and wrapped itself slowly around the brickwork. In the security control room, the cameras failed, the supervisor dismissed it as a blown fuse and radioed Luke to investigate.

The figure in a black smock darted around the basement areas. He doused everything with fuel and discarded the carriers. He then set light to boxes of stock in the cages and the bins. Quickly, the corridor filled with smoke. There were smoke detectors, but for some reason they weren't working. The corridor had heavy fire doors at each end and at the base of several of the stairwells that led to shops and the car parks overhead. The smocked intruder wedged the doors open with rubbish from one of the bins, allowing the smoke to climb up the staircases and into the rest of the building.

Luke noticed the smoke as it entered the shopping centre through the staircase beside the glass lifts. When he realised the building was on fire and the alarms hadn't activated, he radioed into his supervisor to get some help. Against his better judgement, he used his jumper to push the fire door open. He reasoned it was only smoke and there wasn't a lot of it. As the building was empty, he made a snap decision to quickly check downstairs, to see how bad it was. Crouching down as he moved down the stairs, he tentatively took a few steps down and then a few more. He got to the bottom of the stairwell and saw that the doors had been wedged open. Something was wrong, but he was convinced he could save the building.

He moved into the corridor and looked both ways. Smoke from the fires clung to the ceiling and disappeared up the stairwells. Air was sucked in through large vents from the loading bay area. He noticed the discarded fuel carriers. He coughed and spluttered as some of the smoke dried the back of his throat. Luke could see that there was no way he could tackle all the little fires, or close all of the fire doors in time. As he turned to head back up the service stairs, he noticed something odd. In the corner of his limited vision down the corridor, he noticed a door close. He didn't remember one being there before. It was peculiar as that wall backed on to the lorry-loading bay and there were no rooms or offices there. He blinked his eyes to look again for the door, but the smoke now become uncomfortable, weighted with the smell of burning plastics. An electrical junction growled and sparked into flames.

Luke knew it was time to leave. He yanked at the rubbish that held the door open and bolted as fast as he could up the staircase. He emerged in the shopping centre and ran as fast as he could to the nearest entrance. Behind him, he heard explosions and crackling. Apart from a lack of light, the interior of the building seemed undamaged, but that was all about to change. As he exited the building, he could see his supervisor waiting impatiently outside, looking for the emergency services.

* * * * *

Maurice was upset about getting caught again. He told Mead that every time he was released from prison he'd promised himself that he'd keep his nose clean, whatever hardship it meant. As he sat in the middle of his cell and looked at the four walls, the custody sergeant noticed he was sad.

"Did you say he was on suicide watch while he was inside?" he asked Mead.

"He said he was on the same wing as the suicide watch. I never had a chance to ask him. Shall I take him in a cuppa tea and ask him why?"

Mead gathered up some documents and slid them into an envelope. "Nah, he can't harm himself in there. We've enough paperwork to do."

"I'll run these upstairs for processing."

"Thanks."

The young detective swiped her card, entered her code into the keypad and made her way up the stairs.

The sergeant turned to the constable who'd been mopping the custody suite floor, "Good job, now you've done that, it's time for a cuppa. Do you want to check the cells or make the tea?"

"I'll make the tea, Sarge, it must be my turn." He made his way upstairs.

After a short while Mead called down to say that New Meadows Shopping Centre was reported to be on fire and officers had been despatched to investigate.

After checking the empty cells, the sergeant checked over the fingerprint machine and breathalyser. He had his routine if there was a major incident. He looked at the clock, it was about twenty minutes since he and Mead had taken Maurice's prints, completed his paperwork and locked him in.

"Hey, can you watch the desk?" he asked his sergeant. "I need a pee."

The sergeant flipped up the counter and sat on of the two stools.

Bedford pressed the entry buzzer and waved through the window. The Sergeant pressed his release button under the counter, and allowed him into the suite.

"Where's your card?"

"I knew you'd be asleep, so I rang the buzzer," he joked.

"Cheeky bastard!"

"Yeah sure." The detective lifted the counter and started to look around behind the desk.

"Why didn't you get called to the fire?"

"Piss off! I've already done ten hours today, I was just about to go home. It is a Bank Holiday after all. I only came down here to look for my glasses," he said, holding up his missing glasses.

"Part timers!" the Sergeant chuckled.

Bedford sat on the other stool, and began a crossword.

"If there a fire at New Meadows, the ring road will be murder, I'll hang here for twenty minutes if it's okay."

"I'll just check my emails. Don't mind me."

* * * * *

After about ten minutes, the door clicked and the constable reversed through the door holding two cups of tea.

"Quiet, Sarge?"

"Quiet? I didn't think you had anyone down here," Bedford replied, looking up from his crossword.

"Maurice... he's still in number four."

"Do you want me to check on him?" asked the constable placing the teas on the counter.

"No, I'll do it. You drink your tea. I'm in no hurry if there's a fire." Bedford put down his paper, lifted the counter and crossed the floor to the cells.

The constable followed selecting a key from a bunch of about ten.

Bedford slid the inspection peephole cover across.

He saw Maurice sprawled out lifeless across the floor with a surprised look on his face. His throat was cut and his eyes stared toward the door. His head was surrounded by a halo of red as his blood had pooled around his body. There were no entry or exit points and no murder weapon.

"Oh... My... God!"

* * * * *

"What?" exclaimed the sergeant.

"Better call the DCI. It looks like our murderer has struck again."

"You are joking!" he replied in disbelief.

The constable opened the door so they could both see everything.

After a short while, there were other officers in the custody suite, filling in paperwork and rewinding back the video tapes. Bedford and the sergeant were instantly cleared of any suspicion as the tapes showed Bedford doing a crossword and the sergeant at the computer. They were unaware anything happened in the cell. Bedford took charge and escorted the DCI into the cell.

"As you can see, it's got all the hallmarks of the other murders. The victim has been murdered but there's no entry or exit."

"Don't touch anything. Forensics will dust for prints before we move him."

"I'm gonna bet you won't find anything."

"How can this happen?" asked the superior officer. "I've never seen anything like this."

Bedford kneeled beside the wall where the door had been.

"And here is some brick dust."

"Behind that wall is another cell!"

"I know."

"An empty cell."

"Yes, Sir. Cell three, I have no explanation."

"Have you had the analysis back for the dust in the prison cell yet?"

"No, sir. I'm still chasing."

"Compare it with this, and let me know your findings."

"Yes, sir."

"And he couldn't do this to himself?"

"No, Sir,"

They turned to leave the cell.

"There's no weapon."

"Get forensics down here, there must be something here we haven't noticed. Get some photos organised, inform the family and find out where the coroner is."

They left the cell.

McCallum entered the custody suite. He announced that the fire was now extinguished at the shopping centre and that he'd left a couple of constables checking tapes and working with the other services to clear up. He addressed the DCI. "I had a good look around. It looks like arson, there's petrol cans and it looks deliberate, but we couldn't find any entry or exit point. We couldn't find any suspects, the swine's were away before we got there."

"No entry or exit?" Bedford raised his head in interest.

Everyone looked at each other in silence.

Bedford got up from his seat and made his way to the door.

As he reached for the handle, McCallum asked, "Can I see your case notes? I want to know more about this painter suspect."

"Guido wasn't a suspect, we didn't have anything on him."

"Until we understand how this happened, everyone's a suspect."

"Yeah, sure."

Bedford left the custody suite.

"Any gut ideas?" the DCI asked McCallum.

"No. I'll go through Bedford's notes with him to see if we can join any of the dots."

"Good idea. I can release Mead as well if you need some help."

"Yes, I agree. She sat in on the last interview with De Fethney before he died."

* * * * *

McCallum, Bedford and Mead moved to the incident room, joined by additional detectives whom they briefed on the investigation. They sat around a conference table and sifted through all the statements and crime scene images, hoping to find something they missed.

After about an hour, McCallum got Bedford's attention.

"Did you find any connection between any of the victims?"

"Nah. We cross-referenced where they were from, family background, what crimes they committed, what prisons they had already spent time at... everything."

McCallum shook his head, dismissing an idea.

"Harry, the first victim, wasn't from around here, he was born in Scotland."

"Never came here?"

"No, he lived for a while in London, he got sent down for a string of burglaries in Camden. Quite unpleasant and unsociable by all accounts."

"Did any of them have anything to do with New Meadows?"

"Not that I know."

"I'm not dismissing anything. There was no entry or exit damage. Whoever did any of this was inside or used trickery to walk through walls. Sound familiar? It's the thing that is common to all of these events."

The morning sun blazed through the window picking out dust particles and nearly blinding Bedford.

"Well, I am knackered. I'm done for today." Bedford stood up and stretched. "I'll pick this up tonight, if that's okay with you."

"Yes, of course," responded McCallum.

Bedford made his way to the exit. "See you tonight."

* * * * *

Several hours passed as Mead, McCallum and the additional officers appraised themselves of the whole investigation.

"Here's something... It may be nothing," said one of the new investigators, Inspector Robin Castle.

"Yes."

"I'm looking at Guido's profile, and some information is missing."

"What do you mean missing?" He folded it back and passed it toward McCallum.

"Well, it has his childhood, and then jumps to when he was sentenced to Saltmarsh Prison."

"Let's have a look." Castle carefully passed McCallum the information bundle tied with treasury tag at the corner.

"Look at these page numbers, page four to seven is

missing."

"Maybe they dropped out?" They looked around the table but couldn't find any relevant pages.

"Can you check on the computer and see if those pages have got anything important on them."

Castle sat at one of the workstations and logged in. After a while he reported back.

"Not much on it, anyway," he said. "First offence, breaking in to Whittlebury Art College... Never heard of it."

"That's because it was taken over and renamed a few years ago," replied McCallum. "It was renamed New Meadows Academy."

"Next to the shopping centre? I know that place."

"Yeah, we waste far too much time giving out warnings after the students have been shoplifting."

McCallum paused. "Whittlebury Art College."

"Whittlebury Art College," repeated Mead.

"I'm tired, but someone mentioned that place earlier," he pondered. "Maybe I'll remember when I think of something else."

McCallum read from a statement. "Interview with George Black, prisoner, Saltmarsh. That Guido wound everyone up, no-one liked him. I remember one time 'e had some burnt wood delivered. It was an art package or something. I got some Meccano from my boy, but they took the Meccano off me, 'cos they said I could make a weapon, but they let him keep the burnt wood... He even threatened to go on a hunger strike unless he got that wood... The bastard even sneered at me afterwards." He went on to say he was glad when he left.

McCallum dropped the statement to the table while still holding it. "Burnt wood? What could he use burnt wood for?"

"Dunno, we're not even sure it was Guido?" asked Mead.

"I still have no idea. It's a very complicated case. He was near the end of his sentence, I suppose they didn't see it as any harm. The Meccano can be used to make tools or weapons. I've seen that before."

"I can see why everyone thought he was using voodoo and magic. It's very unusual," said Castle.

"If they hated him so much, do you think he might even be the next victim?" Mead asked.

"I just can't see him as a victim, not in this..." McCallum held his head, deep in thought.

"This fire. I think it was just a distraction, I don't think there was a reason for starting a fire at the shopping centre. Anything like that would pull resources away from the station, and give our murderer a chance to attack Mr De Fethney."

"I found another reference to the door painting as well," added Mead. "Items discharged upon release, coat, top, trousers, pants, socks, keys and coins to the value of one pound ninety-two. And get this... A rolled-up signed canvas painting of a red door. The canvas was in good condition apart from being blackened with dirt or soot around the edges." She read on silently.

"So he did take it home with him," McCallum stated. "This painted door is the key to it all. Somehow there is a supernatural connection. It goes against all my training and experience but I can't see a rational explanation."

"What probation officer he was discharged to? I'd like a word with them."

"He was released six months ago to the one in town." She looked through some attached documents. "As his case was overturned, he wasn't on probation.

They were just supporting his return. There's a statement saying he never even turned up for his first appointment."

"Well, they're not supporting hard enough!" McCallum looked at the clock and then at the mass of documents before them.

They all had other duties, so they packed everything away and left the incident room.

* * * * *

Bedford woke in the middle of the afternoon. Outside in the street, children were playing, but their laughter disturbed the sleeping policeman. He went to the window pulled one of the curtains back and looked out. His curtains were heavy, they cut the light but they didn't cut all the noise. It was an occupational hazard when he worked late. He knew he was still tired, so he went back to bed. He lay down for several minutes unable to go back to sleep. He turned on his lamp. On his bedside table was a picture frame with a family gathering. Bedford stared at his uncle William, his face partially melted and warped by chemical burns. Everyone had a shady character in their family, he never spoke with him, but he was pleased he'd had a hand in resolving the family feud. He reached for his paperback book and began to read. His eyes grew heavy again, and he drifted in and out of sleep while still holding the book. Eventually, he switched off the lamp, rolled over on to his side, and settled back to sleep. An hour passed, maybe more.

A deep thud sound came from the bedroom wall behind him. He dismissed the noise in his half-sleep, the doors and windows of his flat were locked as usual, and he knew he was safe. He often had daytime callers selling things or sharing stories about God. Again, there was a louder thud and a ripple of debris. Bedford stirred and then sat up in bed. There was an unexpected sweet smell of wall plaster. He reached across and flicked on his bedside lamp. It failed to light, he flicked the switch on and off in an attempt to get it working. He could taste the plaster in the air, the temperature in his room seemed to drop and the hair stood up on his neck and arms.

A door opened up in front of him, where there was no door before. He looked in disbelief. He was on the fourth floor of a block of flats, and this wall was an outside wall. Dust and plaster debris fell to the floor on to his carpet.

Bedford sat up in his bed. He stared at the wall. He was transfixed, unable to move.

He rubbed his eyes and woke some more. He'd been reading about and imagining what was happening before him. He moved back in his bed. He was curious, but also scared.

As the wall gave way some more, Bedford could see a room beyond the opening. First, a bandaged hand, then a strange figure emerged from behind the door. Illuminated from behind, the figure moved through the opening into his bedroom.

"Bill!"

"Guido?"

Bedford rubbed his eyes again adapting to the sunlight coming from Guido's window, through the doorway.

"Yes, it's the only way I could see you."

"I told you not to come to my flat. How do you even do all that magic stuff anyway?"

"I hate dealing with bent coppers. I've taken out the people you wanted me to. Now it's time for my payment."

Helen Aird

As a child, Helen was an avid reader, with Enid Blyton as author of choice. As a teenager and young adult, she worked through as much of the Penguin Classics catalogue and the works of J R R Tolkien as she could. Her feminist credentials were honed by reading the likes of Margaret Atwood, Sylvia Plath and Eric Jong.

Married with two young children in rural Northamptonshire, Helen studied, first for an Open University degree, then a professional qualification as a Social Worker, then a Masters degree in Business Administration. While there was no longer much time to read anything other than academic texts, write assignments and take exams, she always managed to squeeze in visits to the cinema and theatre and continued to enjoy reading

Now that her children have left the family home and worklife is no longer the driving force it once was, Helen has the space to explore local and family history, and reading and writing fiction.

Helen is still trying to find her voice as far as storytelling is concerned. She enjoys trying out different writing styles and challenges while she waits for the muse to propel her into producing the literary classic to which she aspires.

Today I Saved a Life

by Helen Aird

They say that when someone commits suicide, although it may come out of the blue for relatives and those closest to the victim, the event will have been rehearsed several, maybe many, times.

You don't top yourself just like that.

To be successful, an element of detailed planning is necessary.

How many ways are there to do it, to end your own life? Too many to list here!

The most common methods are: cutting your wrists, suffocation, electrocution, drug overdose, drowning, hanging, jumping off tall buildings, or bridges and cliffs, jumping in front of a train, or crashing your car.

To successfully commit suicide by cutting your wrists, or severing an artery, you have to know what you're doing. If you botch it, chances are you will be discovered before you die, but not before you've damaged your tendons and affected your ability to use your hands and fingers properly.

Suffocation. Usually done by putting a plastic bag over your head. To stop the air-seeking reflex, victims usually take drugs to knock themselves out so they sleep through the whole thing. So, you need to get hold of drugs, find a place you won't be discovered, get a plastic bag, and probably some duct tape to seal it around your head. Forward planning, that's what it's all about.

Electrocution. Get in the bath and drop in an electric heater plugged into the mains. Simple! But you need to make sure there's enough voltage to kill. Do you know how much that is? No. You'd need to look it up. And what happens to you if you fail? Horrendous burns and nerve damage. Don't do this as a cry for help.

So, do you drown yourself? Not the most popular of methods. You need to find a place to do it where you won't be found and resuscitated. Deep water, or maybe your bath, if no-one is going to call round and find you. And you need a fair amount of equipment to prevent you saving yourself when the natural reflex to seek air kicks in. Handcuff your arms behind your back? Stones in your pocket? How many would you need?

Drug overdose is probably the most common and the most unreliable. Most attempts involved over-the-counter drugs mixed with alcohol, and they don't work fast enough before the person is discovered. If you're not an habitual illegal drug-user, you need to find out how to get hold of these and know the amount that is fatal.

Throw yourself in front of a train. Total obliteration! Now that's what I call a comprehensive method. Of course, you need to find a suitable place, secluded but accessible. Know the train timetable. It's a bit rough for the train driver but you probably don't think about him. You're thinking that the world will be better off without you, that you won't be part of it for much longer.

Hanging – short-drop or drop-hanging?

Shooting yourself – the number one method in the USA.

By now, I suspect you don't want me to continue with these different methodologies – unless, of course, you want to end it all.

If that's the case, I suggest you research methods yourself. The internet is a great source of information. Type in, "What is the best method to commit suicide?" and you'll be given so many options that you'll prolong your life by researching how to end it.

So, on that day, the day I saved a life, had the method been rehearsed?

I was driving down Mallets Lane. There were no other cars about. It was late, but not so late that the trains had stopped running. I'd hoped to make it past the level-crossing before the barrier came down. You can wait at that crossing for a good fifteen minutes if you're unlucky.

It was dark, but as I approached the bend right after the crossing, my headlight caught sight of something moving near the track. There's a gap in the fence, if you know where to look, and you can get right on to the track at that point.

In a split second, I thought, "Should I stop?", then slammed on the brakes and reversed so that my lights shone through the gap. I got out, shouting, "Is there anyone there?" I could hear a crunching on shingle and then, as my eyes adjusted to the dark, I could see a person next to the track. They were positioned so they couldn't be seen from the track, where one step at the last moment would mean it was too late for the train to stop.

"Hey!" I shouted. "What're you doing?"

They turned around with a start. Without uttering a word, they pushed past me, out through the gap, running off down the lane.

I stood watching until they were swallowed up in

the darkness.

How do I know I saved a life?

Well, what else would they be doing at that spot at that time of night? If they hadn't planned it in advance, how would they there was a gap in the fence, a place to stand unseen, a place where the trains would be gathering speed?

A place where, if you stepped out at the right moment, all your worries would be over.

The real question, though, is: did I save their life or did they save mine?

The Queen of Swords

by Helen Aird

1. The Discovery

Cassie stared at the earring she had discovered under the settee. It was a silver long-drop in the shape of a trumpet flower with an amber bead protruding from the centre.

"It would suit someone with a long neck," she thought, "and probably someone young, someone elegant". She tried to recall who had worn it, and therefore, who had lost it. Scanning through the appointments in her diary, she counted ten clients for one-to-one sessions, and the meditation group. Using the mental imaging technique she taught her clients, she reviewed each in turn, but couldn't remember anyone wearing it.

She picked it up and placed it in a trinket-box on the mantle-piece. She ruled out the three male clients, and two older women who never wore elaborate jewellery. "I must remember to mention it when they come this week. I'll make a note in my diary to ask them."

Daniel walked into the room. "Hello, Sweetie," he said, planting a light peck on her cheek. "Have you had a good day?" He dropped his briefcase on the floor and his car keys on the table.

"Not bad, but I've still got a mound of paperwork

to do, session notes mainly, so I must crack on. If you prepare the salad, I'll start on dinner in about an hour."

Daniel nodded as he walked through to the living-room and turned on the TV. "Did you hear about that actor who died today? You know, the one that used to be in that series we liked. Set in Yorkshire."

She knew who he was talking about. After twenty years of marriage, they had a sixth sense between them. She didn't answer, knowing he didn't expect her to, but smiled at the thought of the quiet domesticity of their life and the satisfaction they gained from it.

2. Alison Whittle

Alison rang the doorbell, holding her finger on the button for slightly too long. She was five minutes early. She was always five minutes early. In fact, she had arrived fifteen minutes early, but spent ten minutes smoking a cigarette around the corner. Cassie's neighbour, Roger, always got annoyed when Alison stubbed out her cigarette on his gatepost and tossed the butt into his hedge, and every now and again, Cassie bought him a few bottles of Hobgoblin Beer by way of an apology. She probably wouldn't have if she knew that Roger threw her discarded butts back over the hedge into her garden.

"How have you been this week? Have you been doing your breathing exercises? And have they helped?"

"Yes, yes, I have, and yes, they have helped. Apart from when Nigel's there. He laughs at me when I sit in the lotus position and hold my nose. I don't know why he has to be so nasty, why he can't be nice to me?"

Keen to avoid being drawn into Alison's "why me, what have I done wrong" lament, she said, "Oh, by the way, have you lost an earring? I found one under the settee the other day. I'm not sure how long it was there, but it could have been since this time last week."

Alison touched her earlobe. "I don't think so." She was wearing plain stud earrings.

Cassie opened the trinket-box and took out the earring, its shining silver catching the light.

"No, that's not mine," said Alison. "Let's start the session, shall we?"

Alison shuffled the cards. Cassie cut the pack and took two from the centre.

The Two of Cups Reversed. The Three of Swords.

"These cards indicate an imbalance in your relationship, possibly sorrow and heartbreak."

3. Margot Hill

"I need to know if he's cheating on me!" Margot screeched as she strode in. "Bastard! He said he was visiting his sick sister, but she wasn't sick and he wasn't visiting her! I bet he was with another woman. I'll kill him if he was!"

"Margot, Margot. Stay calm – here, sit down. Let's not jump to conclusions. We'll see what the cards have to say, shall we?" Cassie was used to Margot's outbursts. She was convinced her husband was cheating on her, but the readings showed him to be a loyal and faithful husband and Margot to be needy and very jealous.

"Have you lost an earring?" asked Cassie, taking the silver long-drop from her pocket and dangling it in front of Margot.

"Do I look like a woman who would wear something like that? My taste is more stylish. Why don't you ask his floozy? It's the sort of garish tat that bitch would wear!"

"Don't be silly, Margot. Stuart has never been here, and neither has any woman he's been associated with. Unless you think I'm in cahoots with Stuart and his – what did you call her – floozy?" Cassie's attempt to calm Margot down by making a joke fell flat, and Margot looked as if she was about to burst into tears.

"Come on, let's get started."

She led Margot to the table, and sat her down.

Cassie shuffled the pack and spread it out in a semi-circle.

Margot selected two cards.

The King of Cups. The Nine of Wands. Both Reversed.

"You're feeling quite volatile, a bit moody, on edge, perhaps even a bit paranoid."

4. Sebastian Cole

"Cassie, darling," Sebastian hugged her, and kissed her on each cheek. "How are you?"

"I'm fine, and how have you been, Sebastian?" she asked.

"Bonzo's been unwell this week. The poor swee-tie. He's been right off his food. The vet couldn't find anything wrong with him, but thinks it might be doggy IBS. I've got to try to give him peppermint tea, but he's turned his nose up at it. And George is no help. He thinks Bonzo's attention-seeking. Pah! George's jealous. Anyway, I'm at a turning point. I mean – is George the one for me? Am I just with him because of my low self-esteem? He's so… oh I don't know!"

"Let's see what the cards know about Bonzo and George."

Sebastian pulled out two cards and placed them face up on the table.

The Knight of Swords. The Ace of Cups.

"The Knight is telling me that you are opinionated at the moment – too hasty in coming to a conclusion. The Ace is highlighting your creativity, and pointing in the direction of love."

5. Sally Sutcliffe

"I'm getting married, you see. I've been with Jason since Year 11. I was going out with his brother, but he weren't up to much. Then Jason asked me to go and see this band with him. We had a really good time and at the interval we went round the back for a bit of a snog 'n' that was that. We couldn't go back to his, 'cos he lives with his mum. But he has a van, and we've seen a lot of good times in that van! We've been together four years, then he says, 'Shall we get hitched?' and I'm like, YEH!!! He wants a big wedding an' all that, but I'd rather put the money towards getting a place of our own."

"That's really lovely for you," said Cassie. "Let's see what the cards have in store."

Four of Wands.

Cassie held her breath. That wasn't what she expected to see. "Celebration, good times, a happy and harmonious home environment and good news."

"Well, I've got some good news," Sally said. "I'm pregnant! Jason doesn't know yet, but I think he'll be pleased."

6. Jason Thirlby

"I've not made an appointment", Jason said. "But Sally wanted me to come. You know we're getting married, but it's too expensive. I want to give her a great day, but I don't know how we're going to afford it."

Cassie showed him into her client reading-room.

"First, shuffle the cards, Jason, while you think of the question you want an answer to. Then we can do a reading. The more specific the question, the clearer the response from the cards will be."

She turned over the first three cards.

The Ten of Cups. The Page of Pentacles. The Empress.

"These cards really do signal good news! It looks as if you and Sally are going to be very happy together and will soon have an addition to your family. I think Sally would prefer you to focus on her and the baby, rather than a big expensive wedding."

"Baby? What baby? We haven't got a baby. What you talking about?" Jason stood up, knocking the chair over.

"Well," Cassie said, "let's take another look." She straightened each card in turn, playing for time while she revised her interpretation to hide what she already knew. "The Empress is the classic card for pregnancy and fertility and, coupled with the Ten of Cups for harmony and marriage. I expect you will be hearing the patter of tiny feet before too long." She looked up and smiled. "Isn't that what you'd like, Jason?"

Jason picked the chair up and sat down again.

"Well, yes, I suppose so. I mean, I'm not expecting it straight away. We need to get ourselves sorted. I don't think Sally would be too pleased to live with my mum."

"It could be a new job, or a promotion. The Page of Pentacles points towards that. Or a windfall?"

"Well, I have got a tip for Saturday," Jason said. My mate's mate's a jockey 'n' he'll be riding it. A 100/1 outside chance. If it comes in, a pony would net us two 'n' a half grand."

7. The Disappointment

"How's your day been?" asked Daniel without waiting for an answer as he dropped his briefcase on the floor, car keys on the table, picked up the TV remote control and flicked through the channels to bring up Sky News. "You been fiddling with the TV again, Cassie?"

"I haven't touched the thing," Cassie called through from her study. "It must be where you left it."

She came through and wound her arms around Daniel's waist, pulling him in to her. "Mmmm, you smell nice, what's that?" she asked.

Daniel didn't look away from the television as he untangled himself, and stepped to one side. "The University's on the local news. We've bagged a ground-breaking partnership with Shanghai University's Department of Biological Engineering. Ten years I've worked towards this. And now it's going to happen. I'll be able to get my Research Centre set up on the back of this."

"I'm so pleased for you, Dan! You really deserve it after all the work and long hours you've put in. Let's go out and celebrate!"

"Sorry, Sweetie," he said, not taking his eyes off the TV. "I've only called in to shower and change. I said I'd take Cheng and the gang from Shanghai out for a celebration. Just our team. There'll probably be a formal congratulatory dinner with the Vice Chancellor in a week or so. You'll be invited to that."

Cassie turned away.

"You're not disappointed, are you?" he said.

"No," she said. "No, of course not. I'll only be in the way."

Daniel shrugged her off. "You're so understand-ding, Cassie. Whatever would I do without you?"

As Cassie sat at the table smoothing down the purple silk cloth, she battled back her tears.

8. The Group

There was a good turn-out for the Tarot Visualisation and Meditation Group. Of the eight attendees, there were only two she hadn't met before.

"Hello, everyone," Cassie addressed the Lycra and tracksuit clad participants. "Lovely to see you. There's a couple of new faces, so let's go round and introduce ourselves."

"Hello everyone, I'm Sebastian. I've been coming for about three years. It's calming."

"I'm George, Sebastian's partner. I'm a social worker. This is my first session."

"My name's Jason. I've not done this before, and to be honest, I'm a bit scared about meditation. But I'm prepared to give it a go. And… I'm going to be a dad!" A proud and happy grin spread across his face and the group broke into spontaneous applause.

"And I'm Sally, the mum-to-be! Oh my God, I'm

feeling nervous! But Cassie says meditation's good for the baby."

"Alison. I've been coming for ages. It helps keep my nerves under control. And Cassie is lovely."

"Hi! I'm Natasha. I come here for peace and harmony, and to create a centre for my life."

"Hello. Lisa. Lisa Lam. I want a bit of peace and harmony in my life. It's my first meditation session."

"Margot. Hill. I get anxious about my boyfriend being unfaithful. For no reason. This helps me take control of my emotions."

"Thank you. Let's make a start." Cassie went to turn on the meditation background music, when a last voice announced:

"Daniel. I work at the University. I've not attended this class before, but I want to try meditation."

"Thank you, Daniel," said Cassie, surprised by her husband's presence.

"Let's lay ourselves down on the mats." Cassie paused while the group complied. "We'll start to let go of our everyday worries. Keep your legs straight, arms out at your sides, hands relaxed… "

Cassie took the group through the session, turning over a tarot card each time she instructed the group to relax another part of their body, and reading out her interpretation of the card and how it aided the meditation.

9. Lisa Lam

"Have you ever had a tarot reading before?"

"No," Lisa said. I'm not sure what I think about tarot, to be honest. But I enjoyed the meditation session the other day, so I thought I'd come for a reading."

"As this is your first session," Cassie said, "I want you to hold the pack, and tell me a bit about yourself. Then, you can concentrate on the question you want to pose while you shuffle the cards. I will spread the pack across the table and you can pick out three cards. Okay?"

"Well, I'm 22 and a post-graduate engineering student. Born in Islington, half-British, half-Chinese. My father's an academic, a professor, and my mother's a clothes designer. They've been divorced since I was about ten and my father now lives in Shanghai. I get to see him about twice a year, when business brings him over."

"Do you have a boyfriend? Any hobbies or interests outside university?"

"No-one special at the moment. I don't want to get derailed from my studies. I hope to become a professor and have an academic career. I spend time at the gym. I like to follow fashion, I get that from my mum, I guess. I've got a bit of an earring fetish, I love buying them. That's about it." Her Pandora teardrop earrings shook as she shrugged her shoulders.

"What question would you like to ask the cards? Think while you shuffle."

Lisa shuffled the cards. "Well, when I said there was no-one special, there is someone... it's only very casual... but something happened. I'd like... I'd like to know where it's going."

Cassie spread the pack, Lisa picked out two cards, Cassie turned over the first.

The Knight of Cups.

She looked up and smiled at Lisa. "Well, this card is what it seems – a knight in shining armour, a charming man, and romance is in the air. You could be swept off your feet!"

The Seven of Swords.

"This can refer to something that isn't ethical, or someone who is getting away with something, who is deceitful, a betrayal. Looking at it in context with the first card, I would urge you to be cautious about this new man in your life."

10. Natasha and Cassie

Daniel had left early and Cassie had no clients or groups scheduled for the day. She lay in bed drinking the cup of tea Daniel had brought her.

"He's so considerate," she thought as she placed the cup on her bedside table and snuggled back under the covers. "At least another half-hour before getting up. Jogging with Natasha. Seemed like a good idea at the time."

"We'll do three miles along the canal towpath, then cut through Beckett's Park, down along the lane running next to the Enterprise Park, and then back along the canal to the car park. About seven miles in all. You up for it?" Natasha always planned their jogging routes.

Ruby, her chocolate labrador, was eager to get going, and barked.

The two women laughed and set off.

They settled into a steady pace allowing them to chat. "So Dan showed up for your meditation class. That's a first. What made him do that?"

"I don't know. I haven't had the opportunity to ask him. He's been so busy on his Chinese project, working all hours. Perhaps he felt he needed a bit of calm in his hectic schedule."

"Hmmph! Whatever the reason, it'll be for his benefit and nobody else's. That's the only reason he does anything."

"I know you don't like him, but surely my husband can take part in a meditation class without your disapproval," Cassie said.

They met up again later in the week for a film and a meal.

"We'll have melon to start," said Natasha, "and I'll have Caesar Salad and my friend will have Spaghetti Marinara, but hold the anchovies. And two glasses of white wine. Thanks."

"Well, I enjoyed the film, even if it was far-fetched. I mean, would you be able to get up and carry on running if you'd just been shot and then run over by a car?"

"Oh, don't be so literal, Cassie! You just need to immerse yourself in the story – suspend belief! Anyway, you needed to get out. It's not doing you any good staying in by yourself while Daniel's out and about."

"Working hard, you mean," Cassie said. "How's the studio?"

"Fine. I've got the new fitness equipment installed. The marketing campaign is about to be launched, which should attract new members. Classes are well booked. The finances are working out. So, yes, it's going well."

"Great, I'm really pleased for you. I'll have to do a reading for you soon. See if the cards point to anything you're not aware of or that you need to keep an eye on."

"Yeah, whenever," said Natasha.

"And what about anything on the romantic front? Perhaps the cards can help you there."

"Oh, stop trying to match-make. I'm happy as I am."

"Okay, okay. I didn't mean to butt in where I'm not wanted."

After the melon arrived, they ate in silence.

"How's your mum?" Natasha asked after they had finished.

"Same as ever! She and dad have taken up salsa dancing. The mind boggles, it really does! Dad salsa dancing!" They laughed at the thought of Bob and Emma strutting their stuff.

"I must go over and see them. It's been ages. And they were so good to me when I first came back to the UK after… after New York." Natasha looked down at the table.

"Tash, I'm sorry. I didn't mean to remind you of… you know, what happened, when I asked about romance." Cassie put her hand over her friend's and squeezed it. "Oh, Tash. New York was two years ago. I wish I could help you move on."

11. Daniel and Lisa

When Daniel came into the café, he saw her at once. "Lisa – darling," he whispered as he bent over to kiss her and squeeze her stiffening nipples. "Do you think a window table is a wise choice?" He sat down opposite her. "I hope you enjoyed the other night as much as I did. I think it's always nice when lecturer-student relationships can be furthered outside the seminar room, don't you?"

"I think I'd had too much to drink the other night," she said. "I was only at that bar because I thought my father was going to be there. He's involved with your Chinese project. You were very generous with the wine. I can't remember what happened."

"You don't have to worry, Lisa, I'm very discreet.

I'd never tell your father about us."

"And why were you at the Tarot Meditation Group the other day?" she added. "I was surprised to see you, but as you didn't acknowledge me, I left quickly. I was confused."

"You'd told me you were going, so I thought I'd see what it was like," he said. "Besides I wanted to see what you looked like in Lycra." He snuck his hand under the table. "Why don't we slip back to my office? It's more comfortable and discreet. I'd love to show you how I can help you. I can be a great boost to a student's career, if I'm treated properly. And I'm sure your father will be very proud of your first-class grades."

12. The Owner

"It's a Pinot," said Natasha, pouring a generous amount into her glass.

"Mmm, thanks. Just what I need," Cassie said, leaning back in the garden recliner. "Your garden is so lovely at this time of year. I don't know where you get the time to do all the work. I see Ruby has found herself a nice sun spot!" She nodded towards the labrador who was lying spark-out on the lawn. "I didn't find the owner of that earring. Shame, as it's really nice. I wouldn't want to lose it if it was mine."

"What earring's that? You didn't show it to me," Natasha said.

"Hang on, I've got it in my bag." Cassie fished into her bag and brought out the earring wrapped up in a lace and embroidered handkerchief. "Here, have a look. One of my clients must have lost it, but I've asked everyone I can think of and no-one claimed it."

Natasha examined it.

"That's mine!" she said. "I've been looking everywhere for it. I was annoyed when I couldn't find it. It's got sentimental value."

"Oh! I found it under the settee. I'm sure I've vacuumed under there since the last time you were here." Cassie took a large sip of Pinot. "I can't remember the last time you came round," she said. "When was it?"

"I came to your meditation group a couple of weeks ago. Maybe I lost it then."

"No, I'd already found it by then. Before that. The last time you came round was when you dropped in a card for me to take to Mum – that was about a month before, near her birthday."

"How is she?" Natasha asked. "I still haven't been round to see her."

"Yeh, they're okay. Driving me round the bend, though. Dad's decided salsa is too strenuous, and mum's having a strop. She's threatening to find a toy boy dancer who'll show her a good time! Parents! They're such a handful!"

"Here, give me the earring," Natasha said, putting it in her pocket.

13. Sebastian Is Getting Married

"Darling!" The obligatory air kisses followed. "It's all official! George and I are going to get married!" Sebastian flounced in. "Pleeeease give me a reading that shows George is the love of my life! You must come to the wedding!"

Cassie smiled broadly. "Sebastian! My intuition says the cards will give a great reading!"

The Ten of Cups!

"Happiness, joy and contentment! Idyllic state of

peace, harmony and love! Sebastian, I think you've found true love!"

"Yes, I'm sure I have! We're in full planning mode. Venue, clothes, table favours … there's so much planning to do!"

Cassie held his hands in hers. "Sebastian, I'm so happy for you!"

"Darling, that man who came to the group. Daniel. Is he your partner? Only I saw him in Jasper's Coffee Shop with a young girl. Maybe twenty. I don't want to tell tales, but, well … it looked a bit intimate."

"It was probably one of his students," she said dismissively. "He's always having to counsel them about one thing or another. Usually affairs of the heart, rather than academic work. Daniel's always saying he should introduce tarot reading at the selection stage to see if he can weed out those who won't complete their studies due to emotional instability."

"Well, he was certainly counselling her about one thing or another when I saw them."

14. Margot Is Less Suspicious

"You know," Margot said. "I've been coming for readings for quite a while now, on and off. And usually it's because I'm suspicious of Stuart, and the cards always show that I'm wrong. You're always singing Daniel's praises, saying how considerate he is. He seems to work long hours, though, doesn't he? You don't actually spend much time together, do you? It seems to me the only thing he does for you is bring you a cup of tea in the morning." Margot waited for Cassie to answer and when she didn't, continued, "Have you done a reading for yourself?"

61

"Daniel and I are fine, thank you, Margot. Let's remember the focus of this session is on you, not me."

"I don't mean to poke my nose in, it's just that, after all this time, I'm finally starting to see that I'm wrong to be so suspicious. Perhaps you, too, need to look at things from a different perspective?"

Cassie turned the top card.

The Nine of Cups.

"This is a good card, Margot, and I think it indicates that you are starting to get over your suspicions and recognise how much Stuart loves you. This card represents your wishes being fulfilled, happiness and satisfaction in your relationship."

15. Alison's Anxiety

"Can you describe in detail something that has made you very anxious this week?" Cassie asked Alison.

"Well, Nigel's mum came over for the day last Sunday." Alison tugged at her earlobe, and twiddled her stud earring. "She's very… demanding. You know, nothing I ever do is right, and Nigel can do no wrong. I spent all day on Saturday planning the meal, getting the ingredients and preparing as much as I could in advance. Not to mention the major cleaning of the house. Everything looked great, and I even felt quite pleased with myself at how well I'd done."

"That's good you felt pleased and proud of what you'd done. It's a step forward, Alison."

"Well, only for a short while. As soon as she arrived she made me move the flowers I'd put on the table out of the house, declaring she'd developed an allergy, and when I served the meal, she didn't eat any of it because she was on a diet, and accused me of trying to deliberately make her fat."

"Oh dear! Overbearing mother-in-law. Let's see what the cards have to say to help you."

The Five of Wands.

"This card shows conflicts, hassles and minor obstacles to be overcome. So let's put your mother-in-law in perspective. You don't see her that often, and when you do she is usually rude and difficult, and puts you down. But luckily she's gone pretty quickly."

The Four of Swords.

"You need to give yourself a period of rest and recovery, and plan how you will handle the situation should it arise again. Try to get to the point where you can constructively challenge her. Especially as she is behaving like that in your own home."

"Some hope!" Alison said. "We spent all day yesterday out buying a birthday present for her. Nigel wanted to get some earrings. Stupidly I said to him I'd seen a nice earring – you know the one you showed me that one of your clients had lost. So we had to trawl around loads of jewellery stores to find a similar pair. He never thinks that I would like a nice pair of earrings. Why doesn't he ever think of me?" Alison pulled at her earlobe again.

"Anyway, we finally found it in Asters – that posh jewellery shop on the market square. And guess what? We saw your husband."

16. Breakfast with Daniel

"Look at this," Cassie said, showing Daniel an advert. "There's a Tarot and Psychic Convention being held at the NEC in Birmingham next month. It's only £20 to get in, and there's loads of stalls – I know quite a lot of these businesses and readers. Do you fancy coming with me?"

"What? Sorry, I wasn't listening." He bit into his toast, then gulped down some coffee. "Where'd you want to go?"

"To this Tarot Convention," she repeated. "I thought we could go together. It's next month. You've not got anything on, have you?"

"Sorry, Sweetie. Got to work for next few weekends. I told you before. I'm working on the bid to get my research centre."

"Oh, Daniel! You said once you'd landed the Chinese deal you'd have more time for me, for us. Now here you are straight into your next project. You'll burn yourself out."

"I know, but you know how unforgiving the academic world is. You go, you'll enjoy it better without me in tow. I'd probably get bored and then get on your nerves," Daniel said in his best little boy lost voice.

"Well, I think I will go. Maybe Tash will come with me."

17. Natasha Is Busy

"Oh, I'm really sorry, Cassie", Natasha said. "I'm volunteering at a charity rugby match, so I can't go. Why don't you organise a trip with some of your clients? Like a loyalty thank you. Hire a minibus and make a day of it."

"That's a great idea, Tash! I think I'll do that, although I'd prefer to go with you – or Dan. Anyway, I'll let you get back to your session planning. I'm going to start phoning my clients, see if anyone's interested."

18. Going to the NEC

Cassie's clients were gathered in the kitchen, waiting for the minibus to arrive. All her regulars had wanted to come, as well as her mother, Emma, and Lisa Lam's friend, Jasmine.

"I'm not sure I know what to expect," George said. "I suppose there will be stalls selling different types of tarot cards. Maybe people doing readings. Psychics. I'll be able to buy Sebastian some runes or crystals. Would you like something like that, Sebastian?"

"Well," Sally was saying, "I'm going to get something for the baby. Perhaps a birth sign prediction. Although, I s'pose if it arrives early or late it could be a different sign."

"I've always had very strong intuition," declared Emma to no-one in particular. "That's where Cassie gets it from. I fancy having my aura read. I need to know that my chakras are balanced and I'm in a neutral karmic state."

"What's she talking about?" whispered Jasmine.

"I don't know," Lisa responded. "Cassie didn't talk about chakras and karma when she did my reading. Perhaps we'll find out what she means when we get to the NEC."

"All right, all right, everyone," Cassie shouted. "The taxi's here – there's eight seats. So can you put all bags etc under your seats and not on the one next to you."

Sebastian and George walked out to the taxi, holding hands.

Nudging Margot, Alison said, "So sweet, don't you think? I hope we get invited to the wedding. I've never been to a gay wedding. I don't think Nigel would come, though. He's not very tolerant."

They giggled.

19. At the NEC

"There must be over a hundred exhibitors here," said Sebastian in amazement. He examined the Exhibitor Guide. "Shall we split up, have a wander around and meet up at the coffee shop, over there at the far end of the arena?"

Encouraged by nods of agreement, he continued, "Sally, do you want to go with Alison and Margot? You cover this section here." He pointed to the guide. "Cassie can come with us, we'll do the middle section, and, um, Emma, Lisa and, um, Jasmine, do you want to form a trio and cover the right hand side? We'll meet up for coffee at 11.30."

20. Cassie's Mother

"I thought I'd rescue you from going round with your mother, Cassie darling," Sebastian said to her in a mock whisper. "You looked as if one more word from her and you would be driven to kill!"

Cassie laughed. "She's not that bad but, after an hour sitting next to her in the minibus, I needed a break."

"Is she staying with you for long?"

"I don't really know," Cassie said. "I don't even know why she wanted to come and see us. Her diary is usually so full. Still, it's nice to have the company, what with Daniel being so busy with work."

"Perhaps you should get your tarot cards read" Sebastian suggested.

"Oh, no, I don't think so. I don't like having my

cards read by others, and I'm no good at reading them for myself. Funny, isn't it?" Cassie said. "I'm hoping to find some good tarot interpretation books and maybe some different decks. It's good to keep up to date with new developments. Better for my clients."

"Oh, okay. What do you want to do, George? I'm going to put my name down for a reading by Madame Le Fondre. The guide says she specialises in gay readings."

21. Emma Is Suspicious

"So, girls," Emma said in her favourite aunty voice as she linked arms between Lisa and Jasmine. "Where're we going to start? Do you want to do anything in particular? I'd like to look at the Healing Crystals stall, and have one of those mini reflexology foot massages. Jasmine, have you had your tarot read before? There's quite a few stalls offering a simple reading."

"Isn't that disloyal to Cassie? Getting a reading from somebody else. After all, it's like taking trade away from her?"

"Oh, you're a *loyal* customer, are you?" Emma said. "Well, I'm sure Cassie won't mind. After all, she did organise the trip. Let's all get a reading, but from different stalls, and then we can see if they're up to Cassie's standard. We can give her some feedback about the competition!"

Emma manoeuvred Lisa and Jasmine towards a stall decorated with fruit, vegetables and sheaves of wheat. "Organic Tarot, whatever next!" she said, pulling out the chair in front of the stall and nudging Lisa into it. "My friend would like a reading, please. She wants to know whether romance is in the air,"

Emma announced to the woman behind the table.

"Hello, Seekers. I'm Madame Récolte. I have an affinity with Nature and Earth. I believe we must all be in harmony with each other. If we respect nature, nature will respect us. If we lead a good and natural life, our journey will be fruitful and our life-force strong. Shuffle the cards, dear, and turn over the top three. These will reveal Your Current Situation, Your Innermost Desires, and Your Future Prospects."

Frowning with concentration, Lisa shuffled the cards.

As Madame Récolte read out the names of the cards, she touched each with her left forefinger, her right middle finger touching her alabaster smooth forehead.

The Page of Swords. The Wheel of Fortune. The Lovers.

"You are young and have a lot to learn," she said. "You are easily taken in by false promises. Your father is a distant figure, unobtainable, and you hold up potential suitors to the mirror of your father."

Madame Récolte touched the next card. "You have a true and pure heart. You want to find someone who is reliable and romantic. Your idealism and trusting nature leads you to unsuitable partners, but your inherent morality lets you question their appropriateness, and find answers to your dilemmas. You will not be swayed by anyone who is morally lacking."

Lisa stared intently at the third card.

"You have met someone already, but you don't yet know that this is the love of your life. It's not a traditional union, but it is not dishonest or tainted. It will be a while before you realise what you've got. To achieve this you must trust your gut instinct and turn away from your current distractions and focus on your purity of spirit." Madam Récolte concluded. "If you leave your email address I'll send you a transcript of this reading, it's included in the price, and a voucher for a half-price follow-up."

"Oooo!" exclaimed Emma, the edge returning to her voice. "You already know the love of your life! I wonder who it is."

Lisa looked down at the floor, blushing. "I've no idea... I mean, there was someone, but I discovered he was lying to me. He was older. He seemed genuine and considerate, but... And now, I don't know if I can trust my feelings."

"Don't think about that bastard! Think about the mystery person you already know. Who'd you think he is?" Emma gave Lisa a little hug. She now knew Lisa was too decent to try to lure Daniel away from her daughter.

22. Jasmine

"Ahhhh, Jasmine! Sweet, sweet Jasmine! Let me tell you your story." The Sultan held Jasmine's hand as he spread the cards across the black silk table cloth, and tagged one card with his free hand. He turned it over.

"You know, it is interesting you chose this pack. It's a non-traditional one based on precious, semi-precious and gemstones. They look into your unconscious and reflect back the aura of the stones. Ah! The sign of the sapphire. A strong card. You are a strong woman. You know what you want, but you are hesitant to reach out and get it. You are frightened of being rejected. Trust in your heart and trust in the person you desire."

23. The Refreshment Break

"For longevity, prosperity and eternal love we must hold our wedding in March!" Sebastian said. "Madam Le Fondre couldn't have given a better reading! And you're all invited as guests of honour. We'll have the tarot group next to the top table. And each table will be themed around a tarot card denoting either love, honesty or purity. Purity! I'm in love with purity!"

"Yes," said George, squeezing Sebastian's hand to calm him down. "We want you all to come to the wedding. It was meant to be. We've bought the most exquisite tarot-themed Hold the Date cards. We'll be sending them out next week."

Alison, Margot and Sally joined the rest of the group.

"Sorry we're late," said Alison. "But Margot was convinced Stuart had infiltrated the tarot readers to prevent them from telling her the truth. We had to stop near the charity stall for retired tarot readers and make Margot take deep breaths."

Emma was her usual indiscreet self. "Well, Lisa here's been told she already knows the love of her life, but doesn't know who it is. How mysterious is that? And my crystal reading revealed I will soon have a choice between abandoning all I currently have and know for a feverously exciting, but ultimately destroying future, or return to my roots and make amends."

"There's a psychic display scheduled in fifteen minutes," Sebastian said, browsing through his guide. "Tobias Hanzi and his spirit guide will contact those who have not yet passed over and impart their wisdom to the audience," he read. "Oooo, that sounds interesting."

"Creepy if you ask me." Sally didn't like the idea of spirit contact.

"Oh, go on," said Alison. "They might have a message for you about the baby. Besides I'd like to see what a psychic is like. Let's go together."

Cassie moved into her co-ordinating mode again. "Let's all go and grab a seat while there's still some left. It'll only last thirty minutes. Just right for the taxi picking us up."

24. Daniel and Natasha

"I see you've reclaimed that earring I bought you," Daniel said. "What d'you think would have happened if Cassie had discovered you lost it when we were in her sacrosanct Reading Room?"

"Dan, you're such a bastard," Natasha responded. "And what are you doing with that student, Lisa? Poor cow! She doesn't even know you're Cassie's husband. If she gets involved with you, she won't know what's hit her. Another notch for your bedpost. It's New York all over again, isn't it? What do I see in you? You're having Lisa just because you can. You don't care what it'll do to her. Or me. Or Cassie! Although it serves *her* right for stealing you from me in the first place." A Scorpio, Natasha held a grudge for eternity. It helped mask the shame she felt for betraying her best friend.

"Well, at least we've got rid of her for the day. A stroke of genius suggesting she goes with her group." Daniel started to unbutton his shirt. "Come here!"

25. The Psychic's Warning

"Good afternoon, ladies and gentlemen! I am Tobias

Hanzi and I am here with my spirit guide Simionce. Like me, he's from Roma-Gypsy heritage. His name means 'harken' and that is what he does for me. He listens out for the echo of words from those who have passed, but not yet passed over, and he brings into focus those who have a connection in the audience."

Lisa clutched Jasmine's hand for support. "Do you think he may be in touch with some Chinese spirits?" she whispered. "I hope they don't reveal anything embarrassing."

"What sort of embarrassing things have you been up to?" Emma hissed. "An illicit affair, perhaps? Or a sugar daddy?"

"Be quiet!" Tobias Hanzi commanded. "This one is odd, very odd. It's for the sister of Paris and Helenus. It is not the case that you won't be believed, but more a case that you don't believe what is going on right in front of your nose. But beware – there is tragedy ahead. If you are not careful, your revenge will wreak havoc on you as well as those around you. Seek counsel, and take the wise course... Thank you, Simionce, for bringing this. It is a very clear message. Does it mean anything to anyone in the audience?"

Cassie blushed, trying to avoid Emma's pointed stare. They knew he was talking about Cassie – or Cassandra, as Emma had named her. Cassandra... sister of Paris and Helenus, cursed by Apollo never to be believed.

26. Betrayal Unmasked

Emma sat at the table covered with the purple silk cloth. "Cassie, darling." She took Cassie's hands in hers. "You know what Daniel's like, don't you?"

"He loves me, mother, he loves me. He's so considerate, he brings me a cup of tea every morning. Come what may."

"Yes. I know you love him. But he's not faithful to you. We all know what he's up to. You're the only one who won't see it."

Emma turned over the top card.

The Tower.

"You know what this means, don't you?"

Cassie nodded. "Disaster, upheaval and revelation."

"Darling, my girl, I've got to tell you a secret that will hurt. It's hurt me to have kept it for so long." She took a deep breath. "Daniel is having an affair with Natasha. It's been going on for ages. That was why she came back from New York. And he's also seduced Lisa, that Chinese student - and many others over the years."

"No! No! You're lying! You've never liked Daniel, and you'd do anything to split us up. Get out!"

Emma placed a photo on the table. Daniel and Natasha at a party in New York. Natasha was wearing a pair of silver long-drop earring shaped like trumpet flowers with a protruding amber bead. Daniel had one hand on her breast, the other between her legs.

27. The Queen of Swords

Cassie carefully selected four cards from the tarot pack. She hadn't performed a reading for herself in a long while, but she felt the cards' soft murmuring voices enticing her to pick them up, caress them and lay them out on the sturdy wooden kitchen table. This wasn't the pack she normally used - less familiar, found at the back of the knife-drawer.

The Queen of Cups.

A petite, serene woman with long blonde hair, clutching a golden goblet. Someone who, although not psychic, has extraordinary insight into the behaviour and motivation of others. Cassie knew the card represented her, both by image and meaning.

She scrutinised the card and interpreted it as a warning about secrets that remain invisible, and the need to pay attention to intuitive thoughts and feelings.

The King of Swords.

A man with a long white beard holding a sword above his head. Daniel, perhaps... or a reflection of her own anguish.

The Ten of Wands.

The number of completion and achievement, the end of one journey and the beginning of another, an indication of a great burden. Cassie sighed and her shoulders drooped.

She stared at the three exposed cards. Were they about Cassie or Daniel? She turned the final card.

The Queen of Swords.

All those evenings he said he was working late, the last-minute trips away for work, the silent phone calls. She now realised that although she had ignored those signs, she couldn't ignore the small gift box containing a pair of diamond earrings, found in Daniel's trouser pocket. And the note: To Natasha, with lust, Dan xxx.

She stood up, turned around and looked down at Daniel. His beard contrasted with the growing pool of ruby port appearing at his side. A large carving-knife jutted from his chest.

Stepping over the body, she called the police.

"I'd like to report a murder."

Jason McClean

Jason McClean is married with two fantastic children who fill up his days with more happiness than he ever thought possible. Name checks for Gaelen and Ariane and his much loved wife, Lyn.

Jason enjoys mountain biking in his spare time and, the older he gets, the bigger the jumps he is completing. He enjoys riding on the roads as well.

With a background in motorcycle journalism (Chief Reporter at *Motorcycle News* and editor of *Inside Line*, the motorcycle trade magazine), Jason wrote the biography of his friend and triple British Superbike Champion John Reynolds, published by Haynes in 2008 (and still available).

Jason is currently writing short stories and building up his voice and writing style for novels. He reads a lot and enjoys thrillers, horror, sci-fi, fantasy and young adult genres.

Apart from that, Jason is a Director at www.thepropertyinsurer.co.uk and likes cinema (a brief spell as a cinema critic when training as a journalist was one of the best jobs in the world), travelling, theatre, eating out, property investing and meeting interesting people.

Deborah's Diary

by Jason McClean

Monday January 5th

I am a Catholic but I don't believe in God.

Judith is Methodist and Rebecca is Presbyterian. Neither of them knows the difference between the churches. They don't even go to church. The hypocrisy sickens me.

Mary is a Catholic. She is very serious about her religion.

Drinking coffee this morning they wanted to know why I don't believe in God. "Because of the evil, death and despair in the world," I said. "I don't think a merciful God would allow it to happen."

They agreed with me. Even Mary. It bothered her what I said. As a Catholic, it is hard to go against the teachings drummed into you from an early age. I know that myself only too well.

I know for certain God doesn't exist because I kill people. If he existed, then I would have been struck down a long time ago.

God would never have let the priest I trusted so much when I was younger do the things he did. Father Mills taught me God does not exist. How many times did I cry for God to help me and be met with silence?

As I grew up, Father Mills told me he wasn't a bad person, just different.

Some may say there is something wrong with me for killing people, but there isn't. Like Father Mills, I'm different, the way blonde hair is different to black. I'm a killer and someone else is a kill.

I enjoy killing. I savour the control and the power.

More than anything, I adore the intimacy of sharing a person's last seconds of life. Being there when they draw their last breath. Watching the life ebb from their eyes.

It's so private, so thrilling. It is more intimate than sex. You can fuck anyone you like any number of times. I know some girls that have had more than one hundred partners. Every partner I find to kill is a new experience and it only happens once. It has real meaning.

In the last two years, I have killed seven people.

Wednesday January 7th

Mary came to the house today for a cup of tea. She brought her son Michael. She calls him an angel but he's nothing of the sort. She lets him away with murder and is far too easy on him.

He is only five years old and is very inquisitive. He wouldn't stop interrupting us to ask questions.

I don't know how Mary or any mother does it. The little brat knocked over my cup of tea and it spread all over the wood floor.

I didn't make a fuss, but what a pain it was to clean up before Matt got home from work. Getting the tea from between the cracks was nearly impossible. I expect the place will stink when the milk sours.

I hate kids. I hate Michael. He needs to be taught a lesson but Mary is completely incapable, she is a hopeless mother and he walks all over her.

Mary was still upset about what I said on Monday. She is having a crisis of faith and wondering if I might be right that God is a fabrication of our imaginations. I spoke about the atrocities in the Middle East. Only a couple of days ago a journalist was bound and had his head cut off in front of a camera, all in the name of God. I said a loving God wouldn't allow that to happen.

She asked me to go to church with her and put the same questions to Father Mills. I hate that old bastard for what he did to me. He still frightens me even now, nearly twenty years later. I can't stand him.

She thinks if I can return to God then it will help her find faith again.

She was so upset I didn't want to say an outright no, so I said I'd think about it.

Friday January 9th

I had to go out with Matt and his work colleagues, Jim and Ruth, to the Duck and Feather.

As they were talking about web pages, downloads and HTML, I decided that I will kill Ruth.

She is very good-looking. I've seen Matt stare at her. They are friendly and I wonder if they have kissed at work? Or maybe even had sex?

She's single. So is Jim. He's a computer geek who follows her around like a lap dog. It's pathetic.

I've never killed anyone connected to Matt and I before, so it is a little frightening. It will be a challenge.

It is very exciting.

As people quite often say, you've got to live a bit (or in my case kill a bit). I've asked Ruth for drinks at our house next Friday evening. Jim and Matt are away working and will not be back until late. She said yes.

I've got to get some wolfsbane ready.

Friday January 16th

It's been a long week but the night is finally here.

Wolfsbane is not easy to find unless you know where to look.

Fortunately, I do know where to look. I have some growing in the greenhouse beside the tomatoes and chilli peppers. Matt leaves the greenhouse to me. I could be growing opium plants and he would never know.

I picked off five or six leaves with my heavy duty rubber gloves. I get a little nervous handling wolfsbane.

I scattered the leaves in the chair where I am going to make Ruth sit and laced the crisps with crushed wolfsbane.

There's the doorbell, must go.

Saturday January 17th

Last night was brilliant.

Ruth brought a bottle of Grenache and the latest Tom Cruise movie. She appeared genuinely happy we were having a girls' night in.

She helped me to get the crisps and wine glasses and told me she didn't like her job and thought computers very impersonal. She blames them for a lot of bad things, from promoting pornography through to radicalising killers all around the world. I agreed with her.

She told me she was sick of designing web pages and wanted a new job working with interesting people where she could make a difference. She was thinking of nursing.

She hadn't a clue what was going to happen to her.

I poured the wine, put the crisps on the table and the movie in the machine. I told her where to sit, it was the best seat in the house and it was eight o'clock. I knew Matt and Jim were due back around eleven so there was a lot to do in a short time.

The movie started out and it was pure rubbish. But Ruth was getting into it and eating plenty of crisps. Touching the crisps was enough to kill, but the way she shovelled them in meant there was going to be a fast reaction. She even asked what flavour they were. She said they tasted nice.

After a minute I said, "What's that on your seat?"

She looked down and was surprised to see the pretty violet leaves.

She picked a couple of them up and smiled at me. "Just petals."

I asked her to put them on the floor and she rubbed them together and dropped them, sniffing her fingers.

I find that if you can get the person to eat and touch wolfsbane, then they are incapacitated within ten minutes and normally dead by half an hour.

She retched shortly after. The symptoms were showing and it would not be long before she was unable to move.

I switched the TV off and asked her, "Are you comfortable?"

She clearly wasn't. Her good humour was gone and she was sweating, but she tried to smile and make as though all was fine.

I went over and lifted the rug on the floor. I had

placed a thick plastic sheet underneath it, the sort you buy at a builder's merchants. I manhandled her off the sofa and dumped her in the middle of the sheet.

Wolfsbane acts fast once touched by bare skin or eaten and she was in free fall. She had very good health to have resisted for the few minutes she had.

She looked really confused but then threw up all over the sheet.

I put on rubber gloves and held her hand through it. I wanted her to know I was there for her.

The grip of someone vomiting her way to death is something very beautiful. Her hand was alive with heat and strength. I knew in minutes it would be dead, going cold and motionless. It is a special feeling to share those final moments and details of life.

No-one else will or can ever share those moments with Ruth. No-one will know what she went through, the feelings and emotions. But I do. Those are now all mine and my life is richer for it.

When she finished being sick, she lay back and said, "Sorry, I might have had diarrhoea as well."

No doubt she had, it is a sure symptom of wolfsbane poisoning. Her voice was weak.

I knelt beside her head and stroked her hair.

She tried to smile again but was in pain so I had to be quick if I wanted her to know the truth.

"I have poisoned you with wolfsbane," I said. "It is quite deadly and you will die soon."

The look of disbelief was so innocent I shed a tear of joy. If she hadn't been so sick, I would have kissed her on the mouth. I felt so close to her right then, as close as two people can ever get. I patted her hand.

She tried to get up but she was so weak all it took was a gentle nudge and she lay back down.

I kept holding her hand and brushing her beautiful

blonde hair away from her sweaty forehead.

She struggled.

I love to see a person fight for life. All of my kills fight for life in the end. It's basic instinct. We are programmed to live and breathe. And she was fighting hard.

Wolfsbane kills with massive heart failure and through her hand I could feel her pulse racing.

I calmed her down and said, "I will never forget you, the first person I personally know that I have killed. You should be honoured."

She fought bravely, clinging to life for another ten minutes after that.

As she fought for every last second, I told her, "All the memories you had as a child. All the happy and sad times as you grew up. Everything you have ever achieved… all will be forgotten."

She cried as she struggled but it was no good. Then I told her that God doesn't exist. I wanted her to know the truth. I told her not to worry. I said, "God has forsaken you but I will give you meaning. I will remember and love you like no other ever could. We are linked together forever."

I don't know if she heard me as her eyes rolled back in her head and her grip went from strong, to spasmodic, to frail.

She died knowing I killed her and that I was the only one who would ever know. She died betrayed, alone and with nobody to give her comfort apart from me. I had complete control and it was the most euphoric feeling. I still feel thrilled now a day later.

I believe she was grateful I was there in the end. I was her friend at the moment of death. All of the people that I kill are grateful to have me there, especially when they realise God has forsaken them.

It was amazing. It was 20.45 when she finally breathed her last and lay still. I hadn't wanted it to end but I felt so horny and was wet. I got up, pushed my jeans and knickers down, sat on the couch and fingered myself. I came in under a minute.

By ten o'clock, she was back in her own house, laid on the floor, puke and shit around her. She was stinking and cooling down. She wasn't heavy to lift from the car; she really was too skinny, if you ask me.

I spilt wine on the floor beside her with some of the poisoned crisps, switched on the television and left.

I got rid of the plastic sheet and my own Marigolds in the recycling centre. It was closed, but I know a way through the back fence cut open by tradesmen for after hours tipping.

I was home by 10.30 and had to rush to get the room cleaned. I finished off with the air freshener minutes before Matt appeared.

I was still excited and took him straight to bed.

I fucked him good and came again. He must have thought it was his lucky night.

That was one of the best days of my life.

And it kept getting better today.

At around noon Matt got a call from Jim. He'd been around to see Ruth and found her.

It was all terribly sad. Matt was crying and couldn't believe what happened. I played along and made myself cry, though it was difficult, all I wanted to do was smile.

I was the last to see her and said she had gone home early not feeling well. I said she seemed really down and depressed. It turns out they all knew or harboured thoughts she wasn't happy in her job. Jim even thought she might have been a lesbian.

I told them I hadn't thought she would do anything stupid. Matt, Jim and even one of the policemen - Derek Jones - who came to see me, said they understood and I shouldn't blame myself.

I wanted to scream at them I killed her, but their misplaced sympathy was turning me on again. I even forced a little tear or two and went to my bedroom to lie down. I had to put my head into the pillow I was laughing so much.

When Matt came up to see if I was OK, he thought I had been crying. I suppose all tears look the same.

I screwed him again and it was glorious. I took command and straddled him. I used him and when he was spent, I kept going until I was satisfied. I may have hurt him but he is too proud to say anything.

I don't care. I have never felt so alive as I do right now. I shall remember these days for as long as I live, they are glorious.

Friday January 23rd

Ruth's death has hit a lot of people hard. Matt is down in the dumps, which tells me he really did fancy her. She's better off dead for that reason alone.

He had colleagues around and didn't go into work on Monday because he was so miserable. His boss called and told him he needed to be in on Tuesday. Then he really felt sorry for himself. He went in though. He's pathetic.

Killing Ruth has been like detonating a bomb in a closed room. The wreckage is immense.

In the past, I have killed and then got as far away as possible so I could not be implicated. But this time it is close and personal.

Their misery quickens and energises me. Every

time I catch someone with a tear in their eye or a long distance stare, I know they are hurting. I caused that.

I know God has deserted them as well as me. I am not alone.

I can't wait for the funeral. It will be the first time I have attended a funeral of a person I killed.

The police are still investigating and the Coroner has opened an inquest. You can read about it in the paper. I feel a bit famous.

Thursday January 29th

I am getting bored of Matt. He is constantly talking about Ruth and how he couldn't believe she committed suicide.

I can believe it and I want to tell him that. Did he have any idea how unhappy she was at work? How computers made her feel empty?

The living are so selfish when they talk about the dead, they think they know everything. But they don't and the dead cannot answer back and put them right.

Tuesday February 3rd

The police came to see me again. They brought notebooks, pens and lots of questions about the evening that Ruth died.

Matt was at work and I was watching Matthew Wright on TV. They didn't call first to see if I was in. I think they were trying to catch me out. Bastards.

Derek Jones has changed his tune. From commiserating with me straight after the death, he's now asking detailed questions.

"When did Ruth visit?" he asked.

"Eight o'clock," I said.

"Did she seem preoccupied? Did Ruth tell you she had any problems that day? Had she fallen out with a colleague or was she having trouble with other friends?"

"No," I said. "She did tell me she wasn't happy at work and was looking for another job. She certainly didn't seem suicidal about it though."

"What time exactly did she leave?"

"She only stayed an hour, she left around nine o'clock."

"Did she have a car or call a taxi?"

"I don't know, she said she had to go and then left in a hurry."

"What movie did you watch?"

"The new Tom Cruise one, we never finished it. There it is over there beside the TV," I pointed.

"Do you know what wolfsbane is?" he asked and stared me straight in the eye. I was ready for it and didn't look away.

"It's a poison isn't it? Is that what she used?"

"It's just a line of enquiry that we are following," he explained.

After about twenty minutes, they wished me a good day and left. I told them I'd be happy to help if they needed anything else.

Friday February 27th

The police visited again. It was all quite formal but, as soon as they asked to come in, I knew I was off the hook. If they had found anything and suspected me, then they would not have asked. They would have arrested me instantly.

Derek Jones sat with a cup of tea and explained the Coroner had closed the inquest into Ruth's death and recorded a verdict of suicide. They had found traces of a deadly poison in her body and on her fingers. The Coroner believes Ruth knew what she was doing.

They asked if I might need some counselling or had anyone I could turn to. I said I was OK. I told them I if I ever needed someone to talk to I had Matt. I saw them out and did a little jig of joy.

Tuesday March 10th

Today was Ruth's funeral.

I dressed in black and we got to the crematorium at around eleven. The service started at 11:30 but before it, we were invited to look in the coffin.

Matt didn't want to but I did, so I dragged him along. Ruth looked like a picture, as though she was in a peaceful sleep.

I remembered her last moments and they were anything but peaceful. I had to stop myself from giggling by holding a handkerchief to my mouth.

The service was very sombre and lots of people were crying. I could taste the emotion in the air, as thick as honey. It was delicious.

I got to meet her parents - Jack and Jill. I nearly laughed out loud at their names but they were in a really bad state. Jill was wearing make-up to disguise the bags under her eyes but there was nothing she could do for the bloodshot look and the shaking hands.

Jack was as poorly but he didn't have make-up to help. His skin was pale and his eyes haunted. When he spoke, he didn't focus on anything, he was going through the motions.

"I hope it gets easier," I said. It was the appropriate thing to say but inside I hope they find new depths of despair.

"Thank you," they replied in unison but their faces told a different story.

Things won't get any better for them. That thought comforts me. It's another bonus that I missed out on with my other kills. The people that love them most are injured as well. They will live in misery for the rest of their lives. And in the case of a suicide, they will constantly question why they never saw it coming and if they could have done anything more.

Someone told me that Jill is on medication and suicide watch herself.

Imagine if she killed herself. That would be a double win for me, two for the price of one.

The minister in the service talked about God and walking through the Valley of the Shadow of Death. He talked about fearing no evil as God was walking with you.

I imagined what it would be like to stand up and tell the minster the truth. Tell the congregation that I killed her and had got away with it. That she shit herself and apologised for it before dying. That I held her hand and, in the end, I was the only one she clung to, the last face she ever saw.

The congregation listened to the minister, hoping he could help them understand Ruth's suicide. But he couldn't and his words were fuel on a fire. The pain and anguish intensified as the service wore on. The people at the funeral were in agony. That's something they will continue to feel for years or even the rest of their lives.

That makes me even more convinced that God doesn't exist.

While the minister prayed, I prayed as well, the way I had been taught years ago at Sunday school. I prayed with the same fervour as I had when Father Mills had forced his cock in my mouth. The same sincerity as when Father Mills was inside me, tearing my flesh and making me bleed blood that no ten-year-old should ever spill.

I challenged God to strike me down. I told him if he did exist, he was evil for allowing bad things to happen to good people. I called him out in his own house and he did nothing about it. He forsook me. He forsook Ruth.

God is a sham. And with every killing I prove it again and again.

But as ever, there was no response from God. The tears kept flowing around me.

I left the church feeling charged with new energy and vindicated for killing Ruth.

Matt was sad though, he dragged his feet and dabbed his eyes with his shirtsleeve all the way home, saying very little.

When we got home, I tried to perk him up. I wore my lace lingerie and undid his fly while he was sitting on the sofa watching the news. It was the same sofa that Ruth sat on and that got my juices flowing. But he wasn't in the mood and couldn't get it up.

I ended up going to bed early and pleasured myself while he wallowed in self-pity. It was OK but would have been better with him. I resent him for staying downstairs and being miserable. I am seeing him in a different light now. He is becoming a dead weight around the house. Do I need him?

Thursday March 12th

Everyone is still down about Ruth's suicide. Jim is starting a charity in her name to help people who feel suicidal. It's such a politically correct thing to do. "Oh, we've had a tragedy, let's start up a charity."

I read somewhere that there are 160,000 charities in the UK. Another one is hardly going to make a difference and I am sure it will vanish into obscurity in a year or two when everybody gets over themselves and Ruth is a distant memory. What a waste of time and effort. Why bother?

Ruth was a tart who was going to abandon her job and friends as soon as the next best thing came along. I feel better now she is dead.

Thursday March 19th

Things are getting back to normal.

It's been two months since I killed Ruth and it feels a long time ago.

Normally I go three to six months between killing someone. I've done it lots of times without any problems and each kill sates my appetite.

But now I feel empty. I imagine this is how a heroin addict must feel when she has missed a few days of injecting. The colour has gone out of the sky and in the pit of my stomach is a primal hunger.

I have thought about this a lot. I think it was because I knew Ruth personally. I didn't know her well or even like her, but I did know her from social evenings and saying hello when she answered the phone at Matt's work. That's why the buzz, the high from killing her, was so much more intense.

And then to witness all the pain, grief and sorrow rippling out among her family and friends made it even better. I was getting new highs every day. Whether it was Jim on the phone crying to Matt saying he should have seen it coming, or the flowers her parents sent me with a little card saying, "Don't blame yourself. Ruth counted you as a good friend and we are glad she spent her last hours with you."

That message was a new peak for me. They were going out of their way to make me feel better despite their own pain.

But now the highs are wearing off and, as Ruth's family and friends go back to work and get on with the business of earning enough money to live, I am left empty.

I need to kill again.

This is where it gets difficult, though. I don't want to kill a random person. I want my next kill to have intense meaning and to experience the same vivid emotions and ripples of cause and effect as Ruth's death.

Reflected in all the pain and sorrow is the proof that God doesn't exist and has abandoned not only me, but them as well.

I am looking at Matt and wondering if I should kill him. He would be shocked, especially if I confessed to my previous murders while he was dying. He would be powerless to do anything about it and would die in absolute torment.

It is an instinct as strong as the need to breathe. I need to kill.

I don't think I love Matt. I don't think I love anyone apart from myself. I think if most people examine themselves with brutal honesty they would realise this is a core truth. We don't love others, we use them and get used to having them around. There isn't a person that I would not relish killing slowly and savouring their death.

I don't want to be caught, though. I don't think anyone would understand why I do what I do. There are not many people like me. In this way, I am special.

Monday March 23rd

Happy 29th Birthday to me.

It was as dull as ever. Matt bought me a bunch of wilted flowers from the local petrol station. I cooked a cheap night-in-for-two meal and we had second-rate sex before turning the lights out before eleven.

I lay awake for ages. I am so tempted to kill Matt.

Every time he tells me he loves me or does something nice, it makes my imagination fire off with how he would react if he knew what I was really like. He probably would refuse to believe it even as I killed him and he drew his last breath.

The days are so boring now. I know I'll not be able to wait long before killing again.

Mary came around and brought Michael. He didn't spill any tea this time but he left chocolate handprints all over the coffee table. He blamed me for not having a Playstation, X-Box or iPad for him to play with.

Why should I have any of these things? I would be happy if he never visited again. If I never saw Mary again I'd be even happier.

She is very insecure and continues to question the existence of God. She is now using Ruth's suicide as another stick to beat herself. If there were a God, then he wouldn't have let Ruth suffer in silence. "Ruth was such a nice girl," she says.

I genuinely agree with her. If God existed, then Ruth would still be alive as he would have intervened and stopped me from killing her. But he didn't and therefore he doesn't exist.

God didn't show up for my birthday.

But she has persuaded me to go to Church with her this Sunday for Mass. She says if I go with her, then it might give her the support she needs to find her faith again. She thinks if I can find God, then maybe she can find him.

All I will find will be the perverted old priest I hate. But I am keen to help her to realise God doesn't exist, so will play along.

Sunday March 29th

I went to church with Mary and Michael. Matt stayed at home. He's not at all interested in religion, except when he talks about marriage and kids. He wants a church wedding. If we have children, he wants them to go to church.

I don't want children and if I did I certainly wouldn't want them going to church. Father Mills is not the only paedophile; it's a breeding ground of depravity, corruption and perversion.

I do wonder if I could love a child of my own? Would I love my own blood? Maybe. Probably more than I'd love Matt.

If I were to kill Matt, in his last breaths I bet he would be interested in God. All of my kills find God in the end.

But I can't find God.

Every time I am with Matt I can't help imagining him dying slowly and painfully in my arms. It may sound strange but it makes me horny. That gets confusing. I don't know whether I want to kill or fuck him.

We went to the St Joseph and St Etheldreda church on Lichfield Street. It has lots of old traditional character with big stone walls and heavy tiled floors mixed with carved oak pews and brass decorations.

I could make a nice house out of that church. I'd keep some of the pews for effect in the living-room but totally remodel everything else.

I recognised few people that came to the service. Everyone was solemn and serious and spoke in hushed voices, as if afraid to wake some sort of monster.

The only monster in the church is God himself. He commands obedience and complete servitude and in return he allows me to kill his flock. He allowed Father Mills to fuck me as a child. The same Father Mills who preached from the pulpit today. There is no justice.

As Father Mills droned on about how much mercy and forgiveness there is with God, I almost laughed aloud. It was as if we were sharing a private joke, him and me.

When I kill, there is no mercy, no forgiveness. Part of the control is taking everything away from the dying person. Strip them of all hope, humanity and values. Let them know they are utterly alone. That their life has meant nothing and will be quickly forgotten, they are going nowhere, there is only eternal death and emptiness.

Ruth had told me she wanted to move on to a new job and life. As she was dying, I told her, "I will tell your friends you were abandoning them, that you couldn't care less about them."

Her eyes went very wide.

"I will let them know the spineless liar that you really were. They will believe me as well, I am the last person who ever spoke with you. They will hate you. They won't even go to your funeral. I will, though. I'll be there. I won't miss it. We have a special connection now. I'll watch as they burn your body to ash. I can't wait."

She sobbed at that. I was proud of the words I had used.

At the end of the service, I stood with Mary and the old paedophile Father Mills joined us.

"And how is Michael doing at school? What year is he in now?" asked Father Mills.

I wondered if the old priest was hoping to bugger Michael at some point. The priest screwing Mary's little angel would not surprise me.

"He's in reception, Father," smiled Mary. "He's learning to read now, it's amazing."

"And what about you, Deborah? Any plans for marriage and maybe children?"

"Not at the moment," I said.

"Well, maybe we will see you come back to church, we have missed you," he said. "You know God's door is always open to you."

"I have been knocking on God's door, Father, but I cannot find him. No-one is home, if you ask me."

"Oh, child, God is testing you, seeing how you act. Everything you go through is a test and one that I know you can endure. Trust me, he wants you to come back to him."

He paused and looked me in the eye, "I want you back, Deborah."

That threw me off balance.

"I feel as though my sins are too deep for any forgiveness," I spluttered.

"That's a good start, child," he said. "You know the magnitude of your own sins and if you feel truly sorry for them, then you will be forgiven. It is written and that is what Jesus Christ died for."

"Will you be forgiven your sins, Father?" I asked.

"I know I will be, child. I know I will be."

The fucking temerity he had, to say that.

There was a pause and Mary looked at me hopefully. But I shook my head. There is no God to forgive me. I have proved it with my actions. Father Mills has proved it with his actions.

"Come to Mass again," suggested Father Mills. "Come and take confession. I am sure you will feel a lot better."

There is complete confidentiality in Mass but he is the last person I would ever want to be alone with in a box.

But the thought of telling someone and sharing my secrets is attractive in a strange way. Only my kills know what I do and they are powerless to stop me.

"Thank you for the offer, Father, I will think on it."

As he walked off to speak with other members of the congregation, I wondered maybe killing him would be even better than killing Matt. I hate him for what he did to me.

How good it would be to kill him slowly, watching as he came to the realisation that the God he thinks is ready to forgive what he did to me doesn't exist? Take his whole world away from him.

If God really did exist, surely he would intervene as I killed his servant? Or maybe God should have already got involved and killed the pervert by now?

He's an old man, so it would not be difficult to end him. He lives by himself on the church grounds and prides himself that his door is always open to the congregation.

There is something very tempting about killing a priest. Especially Father Mills.

I remember his complete tyranny for three whole

years. He showed me everything the church stood for was a sham. He was the devil in God's house and the master welcomed him there.

Maybe I should hit back at the heart of the institution? The church and Father Mills have always frightened me, though. I need to consider what I do carefully.

I will make my decision by next Sunday on who I will kill next. There is sunshine in my sky again.

Sunday April 5th

Contemplating who to kill has given me focus.

But it has got more complicated. There is a third contender.

First: Matt is a simple and trusting soul. There is an innocence to him that attracts me. I know he will never betray me.

His innocence belongs to me because I can never personally be innocent again. The church took my innocence away. In a way that means God has crafted me into what I am today, which is anything but innocent.

Matt enjoys his work and loves coming home and doing things with me. He's forever buying me little gifts, doesn't go out with his friends much and never argues when I want to do something. He's a pushover.

Maybe I do love him. Whatever love means? I have thought it through and think if I were to kill Matt I might actually miss him the way most people miss a puppy dog.

He is the closest person in the world to me. To kill him would not only be his sacrifice, but mine as well.

I think it would be a wonderful experience. It

would hurt me and that would be worth feeling all by itself. I'd like to know and feel that sort of emotional pain.

But that is also the problem. I'm not entirely sure I want him dead. I could grow closer to him over the years and then in a decade or so if I killed him, perhaps it would be even better. A real work of art and passion. So I rule Matt out. For now.

Second: Father Mills is a tempting thought and I do like the irony of killing him while his God abandons him. I'd like him dead for what he did to me.

He called during the week to see if I was going to church today, but I decided against it. He said he would love to come and visit me at home and talk through any issues I have. I don't think he'd want to hear my issues with God and I am sure he doesn't want to talk to me. I wonder if he would try to rape me again. Or is he trying to gain my forgiveness?

Mary wants me to invite him round for coffee.

That coffee morning could be my perfect opportunity to kill him. Use a slow acting poison that paralyses and talk him through his pending death and how God did not give any inkling what was about to happen to him. I think the theological discussion would be remarkable. Would he hold on blindly to his faith or see the truth before the end?

I would have agreed to the coffee morning if it weren't for a third and final contender coming in at the last minute and winning the nomination to be the next kill.

Third: Mary and Michael came round again this morning. She told me all about seeing the light and finding God again. Apparently, her life is so much better now.

"It's all been a test of my faith," said Mary. "When you were with me in church on Sunday, I could see God reaching out for you. He spoke to me, Deborah, he told me that I could help bring you back to him. That's when I realised God was alive inside me and I have a mission to help you back on the road to Christianity."

There was silence.

"I hope you don't mind me sharing with you?" asked Mary, without pausing for my response. "But God has been clear to me. He wants you back and that's why I am telling you this."

I held up my hand and said, "So these are direct conversations God has had with you? He's spoken to you, you've heard a voice and recognised it as God?"

"Yes, that's it, Deborah, exactly." She took my hand.

I smiled and took my hand back. "Mary, you have not heard God's voice, have you? Not the way you hear my voice now, speaking to you?"

"Of course not," she laughed. "Not like this, but I heard God in my head and my heart. It was as clear as we are talking now, I know I have a place with him and he loves me. I know he loves you, Deborah."

There was another silence, longer this time. What could I say?

"I have prayed for you," said Mary. "I told God you are a good person and he made it very plain he loves you."

I was at a loss for words. It seemed so ridiculous. I didn't know whether to laugh at her, shrug it off, be offended or act grateful.

Suddenly, there was a crash from the kitchen and a loud wail from Michael.

Mary rushed in and I followed, still reeling from

her onslaught and how I should respond. I thought I had been clear to her on my beliefs. Maybe I should ask her why God hadn't responded those times when Father Mills stuck his fingers up my anus as a young girl, hand over my mouth so I couldn't scream and all I could do was pray?

Should I have asked her where God was when I killed Ruth?

Michael was in the middle of the room with the biscuit jar burst open and shortbread all over the floor.

My first thought was he had ruined a good packet of biscuits. But he was crying sore and Mary was all over him, so I painted false concern on my face, "Are you OK? Don't worry about the biscuits, I'll tidy them up."

Then I had an epiphany.

Mary and Michael looked absolutely perfect together, the way any loving mother and son do. She was radiant in her faith and happiness in life. She was so caring and loving for her son.

And that's when the third wild card contender came to me.

In that moment I knew with the same certainty she had told me about God existing, that I want to rip God away from her. I want her to know the lie he really is. I want her to know that her best friend - me - is anything but and she has been a fool to confide in me. As I had been a fool to trust and believe in the church and Father Mills, I want to strip her of everything and bask in the aftermath as her life falls apart.

I am going to kill Michael.

Tuesday April 7th

Mary has asked me to babysit Michael on Saturday night. I said yes.

She is going out with a man she met at the church on a date. He's another Christian and they are getting on well.

I think that's hypocrisy of the highest order as she is a divorced single mother and I thought the church (God?) frowned on that sort of behaviour. But the church changes with the times to stay popular and now accepts divorcees. It seems to accept rapists and paedophiles as well. History teaches us it accepts murderers and endorses war. It is such a hypocritical institution.

Michael and I are going to eat crisps and chocolate while watching cartoons.

I can't wait.

I need to find something that will kill him around four or five hours after I leave. It also needs to look completely natural, so there is no suspicion on me.

I'm off to the library tomorrow to do some research on poisons that fit the bill. I use the library so there is no electronic trail on my own computer.

I am sure that Michael's death will shake Mary's faith. I am confident she will suicide. I might even get to help her kill herself.

This is going to make Ruth feel like an appetizer. There is something different about killing a child. I understand that is a significant line to cross. It's going to be special.

Wednesday April 8th

I've been thinking about Michael overnight and the

prospect of killing him has me excited.

All his potential, hopes and dreams for the future will be snuffed out.

It's quite a step up to kill a child.

I spent most of today researching on the internet how to kill him. I made sure I cleaned my cache, cookies and browsing history when I was finished.

Finding something that is untraceable is difficult. I need it untraceable because I am killing a child and the scrutiny afterwards will be intense. I will have been one of the last people with him so it needs special attention to get it right. Chloral hydrate is almost impossible to detect but there is severe blistering on the face. Those symptoms would cause alarm. I've used it before but left the kill under a sun bed without switching it off.

Hemlock is another possibility but will deliver immense amounts of pain in the hours leading up to death. It's natural and could be ingested by accident, but the hours of pain would alert Mary and if she gets Michael to a hospital then it is likely they will diagnose the cause and it could come back to me. And he might live. Neither of those are desirable outcomes.

Oleander, rhododendrons and azaleas are lethal and difficult to detect but the symptoms are violent and obvious. Mary would act before Michael died and that would mean a chance of survival for him and me being caught.

The best-looking poison may be paracetamol. I'd need to make it look like Michael took an overdose by accident. Tylenol is paracetamol in liquid form and if he drank a large bottle of that and then dumped it down the back of his bed to be found later, then he would die a day or two later from liver failure.

It sounds good but it requires Mary to have Tylenol in her house. She's likely to have some but how do I make it look like an accident? It comes with a childproof cap.

Injecting Michael with air could stop the blood to his brain and cause death but the injection mark would be noticeable and certainly draw the attention of a Coroner.

Killing a child is harder than you think if you want to get away undetected.

Thursday April 9th

An accident by definition is an accident. There is no detectable premeditation in it. That is what I need for Michael.

Electricity, gas or water are in abundant supply in houses, so it must be one of them. And I will have to look as if I did my best to save him.

He will not be having a bath with me, so that rules out water.

Electricity frightens me and I have no idea how I could safely kill Michael without killing myself.

So it is going to be gas. Mary has a gas hob and oven.

The problem is that natural gas stinks and it will need to displace a lot of oxygen. It's not like the coal gas from years ago that was lethal to breathe. I'll need to force his head into the oven.

I shall talk him through what is happening.

Once it's done, I'll leave the gas on and, as soon as it gets unbearable, I'll call the police and stagger to the door carrying his body. I'll pass out.

I'll be found near death trying to save the lad. I'll be a heroine. I'll tell them I found him in the kitchen playing with the oven and tried to revive him. Then, when that failed, I tried to get him out of the house.

It's going to be uncomfortable for me to inhale so much gas, but the ends justify the means. Even if I am in hospital for a day or two, the effect of his death on Mary will be catastrophic and worth it.

She'll soon realise God doesn't exist.

I'll write again as soon as I can.

An extract from the Diary of Detective Sergeant Derek Jones

Sunday April 12th

I started my shift as normal yesterday at 1800 and was on my tea break at approximately 2030 when I received an urgent call from colleagues to attend the address of Mary O'Kane in Rugeley.

When I got there I found Deborah McMahon, a friend of Mary's, in the kitchen. I am waiting on the Coroner's report but am certain a single bee sting causing massive anaphylactic shock killed her. I've seen it before.

Mary's son, Michael, aged five, was in the living-room with his mother and my colleagues. He was the only one in the house when the bee sting occurred. Deborah had been babysitting.

Mary agreed I could interview Michael briefly. I was expecting a messed up kid who was going to need psychiatric counselling.

But I got something very different.

He told me Deborah had tried to kill him by putting his head in the oven with the gas switched on.

I asked him how he knew she was trying to do that. He said she had told him what was going to happen.

He said Deborah was a sheep who had wandered from the flock. It was time for her to return to God.

Michael said he tried his best to get her to reconcile with God, he begged her, but she ignored him. He told her that he was an Angel of the Lord and was trying to help her. She had gone to grab him. That was when the bee stung her.

I asked him if he had been afraid and he said no, God was with him.

I felt compelled and asked if God was still with him.

He said yes.

"I am the angel Barachiel," he said. "Michael is an instrument of the Lord. He is blessed."

That frightened me but I couldn't stop listening.

Michael – Barachiel - went on to tell me in detailed terms how Deborah had killed before. There were eight deaths I could investigate. He gave me names.

He didn't speak in the words of a child. He spoke as though he were a father talking patiently to his son. I swear his eyes were not those of a five year-old boy. They burned with fire and righteousness. And love.

I filled pages with notes on the claimed prior murders and then he said, "Deborah wanted to find God and now she has. You are a good man, Derek, but good men do not come to the kingdom of God just for being good. You need to accept God into your life and repent your sins. You are witness to God's power on earth this day."

As soon as he finished that sentence, he smiled and I knew five-year-old Michael had returned. He asked his mother if he could go to bed, he was tired.

I am sure it will go down as a shock response and

he will be evaluated and cared for, but I am convinced Michael - or Barachiel - was telling the truth.

Mary put Michael to bed and told me it was God's will. She urged me to follow up on the murders.

"Barachiel is an Archangel," she explained to me. "One of the seven Archangels of the Lord. Michael has truly been touched by God."

I left the house and I am not ashamed to say I was terrified of what I had witnessed.

It was 0100hrs by the time I got back to the station. I got straight on to the computer to investigate the names Michael had given me.

There were eight names in total and each one of them was killed or a suicide. I have made enquiries to the police forces involved and will follow up through the coming weeks. One of them is a suicide I investigated over the last months.

I finished my initial investigations at around 0900hrs this morning and was going to go home, but I remembered what Michael had said about a diary that Deborah kept.

I accompanied a colleague who was due to go to Deborah's address.

We got to Deborah's home at about 1130hrs and I let my colleague question the boyfriend. Michael never mentioned him. My gut tells me he is ignorant of what Deborah was. He happily let me roam the house and said he didn't think she kept a diary.

It didn't take me long to find it in a drawer underneath accessories and hair bobbles.

With gloves on, I quickly scanned through it.

Deborah's diary is tantamount to a confession to killing eight people. It shows premeditation to kill Michael.

I will be opening an investigation into Father Mills as a suspected paedophile. The diary says he raped Deborah at an early age.

We returned to the station and I passed the diary on to the forensics team to make sure it is legitimate.

There were numerous extracts in the diary where Deborah claimed her murders proved God didn't exist.

When I think of Michael – Barachiel - the night before, the fire in his eyes and the absolute certainty that he was doing God's bidding, it scares me at an instinctive level.

I was shaking with fear. I decided to attend afternoon Mass on the way home at St Joseph and St Etheldreda's on Lichfield Street.

Father Mills was welcoming and generous, everything you'd expect from a priest. What Deborah claims he did to her is nothing any priest or man should ever do to a child. I wonder how many other children he has touched and lives he has ruined? I will find out.

Mary and Michael were there. Michael was playing with a toy car.

I sat beside Mary and she asked how I was.

I didn't know how to answer.

A bee landed on the pew in front.

Michael turned to me.

But it was Barachiel who asked, "Do you believe in God?"

Kim Grove

Being an ex-nurse and district nurse, Kim has changed career direction and now writes professionally, producing several newsletters a month on a range of social care topics for Agora Business Publications. Proof that you can actually make a living from writing!

Kim has a garden design diploma and Royal Horticultural Society (RHS) Gold Medal for a Sensory Garden she designed at BBC Gardener's World Live in 2011 during her diploma.

On the back of this and because of her nursing background, she began designing gardens for people with dementia and has written articles for magazines and journals on this topic.

In addition, she is preparing a book of off-the-shelf dementia-friendly gardens plans and design information for those organisations who cannot afford the costly fees a specialist garden designer commands.

Kim is keen to diversify into fiction writing. Having already written one (unpublished) novel, she is currently working on another and has written many short stories, some of which appear in this anthology.

Kim is a member of the Northants Writer's Ink and attends many of the Literary Festival events held in her hometown, Oundle.

The Empty House

by Kim Grove

Charlotte opened the door and stared open-mouthed at the empty hallway. Gone was the hall runner, the coat stand and the mirror on the wall. She frowned, trying to remember whether she should have known about this. She peered into the lounge, but there was no sofa, no coffee table, no bookcase, no TV. It didn't even look like a lounge anymore. What's happened, she wondered. Where is everything?

The rest of the house was the same. She looked into each room in turn. The kitchen was devoid of furniture, appliances and utensils. The dining-table, usually ready laid with her best bone china and crystal glasses, was missing. There were no beds, the wardrobes had gone, even the bathroom fittings had disappeared.

Charlotte could feel her stomach tighten. She felt sick. Questions were running around in her head, falling over each other.

"Where is everything? Who's done this?" she said, tears falling down her cheeks. "Robbie! I bet it was Robbie."

Finally, she could bear it no longer. "No-o-o-o-o!!" she yelled in anguish into the room, the sound echoing around the silent house.

She heard a distant slam of a door. Her tears stopped immediately. Her heart was thumping in her chest. She cocked her head to one side, and listened as footsteps came closer. The door opened and she spun around.

"Darling," he said, rushing towards her, arms outstretched. "What's wrong?"

She turned waving an arm in the air. "It's all gone! Robbie's taken everything." She was sobbing again.

"No, he hasn't, darling. I've taken it."

Her tears stopped abruptly, her eyes narrowed. "But why?"

"I thought it was time for a spring clean, so I took everything away. We can redecorate it you like. Put up some fresh wallpaper; lay some new carpets or rugs. What do you think?"

A smile slowly transformed her face as the relief sank in.

"Can I choose the colours then, please, Daddy?"

"Of course you can, darling. It's your dolls house."

Tram: San Francisco

by Kim Grove

Holly Golightly scanned the room. It was large, with a high ceiling, bright lights and several white solid pillars on to which you could place your glass or complete your purchase. Stark black and white photographs hung on plain white walls. Ten or twelve people were standing around, champagne glasses in hand; even the blues and greens of their clothes did nothing to improve the cold feel the room portrayed.

Her heels echoed as she walked towards the waiter holding a tray of drinks. His upright stance, starched white shirt, black bow tie and tails reminded her of Anthony Hopkins in *The Remains of the Day*.

She took a glass and sipped. Hmm, Laurent Perrier, she thought as she surveyed the exhibits. It always amazed her how much people would pay for very ordinary art by someone just because they were well known.

Holly raised her glass to a couple of people she recognised, as she made her way to the centre of the right-hand wall. She stood in front of a photograph. Without knowing why, she always started in the middle. She looked at the image, head to one side, caressing her pearls. The other hand nursed her champagne.

She sighed and tucked a stray wisp of dark hair behind her ear, not wanting to ruin the effect she had carefully constructed for herself today. It was near perfect, the only difference being a shorter cocktail dress and the absence of a long cigarette-holder.

The photograph was dreary. A tram on its way to the top of a hill in San Francisco. The two discernible people in the photo were not posing and wouldn't be missed if they were not there. But it was no better than the holiday snap she had taken in San Francisco earlier this year. She lifted her sunglasses and squinted at the caption. *Tram: San Francisco.* Sir David Ingram. £12,500. She replaced her sunglasses, took a small sip of champagne and tried to hide a yawn with the back of her hand.

Feeling she was being watched, she looked around and scanned the room. She saw the young man. Average height. Dark curly hair. Far too long for her liking. She turned her back on him, knowing she wouldn't be alone for much longer.

Sedately, she moved on to the next photograph. *Alcatraz: San Francisco.* Sir David Ingram. Again, £12,500. Hmm. Slightly better than the last. Eerie. Chilling. Cold. She shivered slightly.

She smelt rather than saw the young man as he stood beside her. Too much aftershave. She decided to let him do all the work.

"Do you like it?" he whispered.

"Not really!" she replied. "It's a bit dull. I think I've taken better photographs myself!"

"Oh!" he replied.

Holly slowly turned around and looked him up and down. "Why do you ask?"

"Well, I took that dull photograph," he laughed. "David Ingram." He gave a little bow.

She almost laughed out loud. "Sir David," she said, trying to control her smile, nodding at the inscription beside the photo.

"Samantha Lord." She held out a gloved hand to see whether he would kiss it.

He declined, shaking it instead.

"Did you take all of these?" she asked with a throwaway gesture.

"Pretty much," he replied.

"Well, I'm something of an art critic. I could do with an interview with such an eminent artist such as yourself. How about lunch? Then you can tell me about your work, and maybe I can write up an article or two about you."

"A critic!" He opened his eyes wide and rubbed his forehead. "Umm…what magazine do you write for?"

"Oh, Aesthetica. Art and Antiques. Art International. Any that will have me really. I'm freelance."

"Why are you interested in photographs of San Francisco?"

"Aside from them being by such a well-known artist as yourself?"

"Well, how can I resist such a charming lady?"

"Shall we go? I know a lovely little place just around the corner," she said.

As she finished her champagne, Holly looked around the room and caught the eye of a friend. Smiling, she put her empty glass on Anthony Hopkins's tray and linked arms with Sir David.

* * * * *

"Madam," said the maître d', "how lovely to see you again."

Holly waved the menu away. She couldn't read it without her glasses, and she knew it by heart anyway.

"Delighted to be back, Marcus," she answered, then turned her attention to Sir David. "Shall I order?"

"Why not?"

"Marcus, we'll have the caviar, then lobster frites, followed by your fabulous crêpe Suzette. Could you prepare it at the table as you usually do? Oh, and we'll have a bottle of Laurent Perrier, thank you."

The maître d' gave a slight bow, "Of course, madam," and took his leave.

"It is so good of you to take me to lunch," she said to Sir David. "I don't get out much these days." She watched as his face reddened and he loosened his shirt collar with a finger. "Is everything all right?"

"No...I have to use the bathroom," he replied. "Do you know where it is?"

"It's through there," she pointed.

As he left the table, Holly looked at her watch. Hmm. 12.30pm. She wondered how long he would take.

She amused herself by looking around the restaurant. White table linen, silver cutlery and fresh flowers adorned each table, all reflected in the line of mirrors circling the walls, making it look more opulent than it really was. A couple sat at a small table in the far corner were leaning towards each other whispering and laughing. Another couple were having a very quiet row, arms folded, frowns on each face, their bodies turned away from each other.

She looked at her watch again.

"Darling!"

"Darling!" she said holding out her hand as if he should kiss it. Which he did. "I haven't seen you since... San Francisco."

"Don't be ridiculous, darling. You saw me not

twenty minutes ago. Who are you today? Holly?"

"Samantha Lord. Tracey is far too common and Samantha was all right for Dexter."

"Good grief, darling. Why don't you stay as yourself?"

She craned her neck towards the door.

"He's gone, I'm afraid," he said. "I passed him as I was coming in. You really shouldn't play games with these poor, unsuspecting gentlemen."

"He said he was you," she sighed. "I wanted to see whether he would buy me lunch, or whether he was the same as all the others."

"Well, perhaps, he still can," he said.

"Well, thank you very much, Sir David."

"You're very welcome, Lady Ingram." They laughed as he sat down. "I expect you've already ordered!"

A Different Type of Service

by Kim Grove

I looked up from under the bonnet as I heard laughter coming across the workshop. Sam was talking to two women who had come in to collect their car. I caught snatches of Sam explaining what had gone wrong.

Once again, I felt a flutter in my stomach, which rose up through my chest and lodged in my throat. I felt sick and took deep breaths, until the sensation had passed. I didn't want to recognise these feelings so turned away, grabbing at a spanner from the side of the engine, in a way that a child would grab a comfort blanket.

At first, I'd put it down to my pride in working for someone who was trying to make a difference, to change people's perception of how a garage works. This place was different to the last one, where the mechanics seemed to excel in making people, especially women and older people, feel small. They talked down to them as if they were stupid not to know the ins and outs of a car engine.

I strained to hear what Sam was saying.

"The… had broken and that's… so we've… "

"Oh, right," the shorter of the two women replied.

"So that means… " the other woman this time.

"Yes, and…means we've had to… " Sam replied.

As the voices faded in and out, I remembered the day Sam had interviewed me. I had never had an interview like it. I'd heard some good reports about the garage from several of my friends. So, when I saw an advert for the job of head mechanic, I applied.

When I walked in for my interview, I had quite a surprise. I recognised Sam from school. The dirty blond hair, the blue eyes that always seemed to have a devilish glint in them, but best of all I remembered the constant laughter. Sam was always laughing; in fact, Sam had a loud but infectious laugh that made others laugh too.

"Hi, I'm Graham. I don't suppose you recognise me."

"Well, if it's not Graham Johnson! You were in Miss Day's class, weren't you?"

I could feel the blood rising into my cheeks and put a finger in my shirt collar to loosen it, releasing some of the heat. "Yeesss... " I replied. I could already see the job slipping away from me.

"It was your class that pulled that stunt on Mr Stevens, wasn't it?"

Oh God! Here we go. I held my hands up in submission. "I don't suppose I'm going to get the job now, am I?"

"You're joking, aren't you? We all thought it was great fun. We were laughing about it for weeks. Fancy old Stevens thinking you'd all fallen into the river. He must have been beside himself."

"No! He wasn't happy about it and neither was the Head. We all got detention for a month and were barred from the Christmas disco as punishment."

"I heard! Oh well. He got over it," and, pumping at my hand, Sam laughed the way I always remembered. "Well, how the hell are you?"

"Good, thanks. You?"

"Well, I can't grumble, I've got this place to keep

me busy. It seems to be doing well, too, which I guess is why you're here. We'd better get on with this interview."

Sam went on to explain the philosophy of the place. "What I'm looking to do, is offer a different type of service to our customers. One that doesn't patronise people. Is that something you could sign up to?"

"I think it's a great idea," I said. "I've often cringed at the way some blokes speak to people, women in particular."

I got the job. Sam offered it to me as soon as the interview had finished, saying that most of the applicants seemed a bit fidgety about this approach. One of them had even gone so far as to say the garage would close within three months!

He was wrong. The garage was popular. Women used it and their husbands and boyfriends, were willing to indulge them.

Each day the work was much the same, but I could feel a change coming over me that I was trying to ignore. I couldn't eat, picking at the food Katie made for me, and my hair started to fall out. Every time I saw Sam, my stomach churned, my heart beat faster, my groin ached. I didn't know what to do. I had started pacing around the house, and Katie was questioning what was wrong. Of course, I couldn't tell her.

Whenever Sam asked me something, the words wouldn't come out of my mouth in the right order and sweat glands in my armpits burst into life. I tried to judge whether Sam felt the same way, but I couldn't tell and I wasn't ready to blurt it out. *How do you approach something as sensitive like this? I mean, Sam was my boss. It could cost me my job.*

"You alright, Graham?" Sam said to me one time, frowning. Another time, "You're looking pale, don't you feel well? Go home if you want to." Did I imagine that look of concern? Was I seeing reciprocal feelings? Or was I reading more into Sam's concern than there actually was?

Anyway, so there I was, listening to two women laughing with Sam. Once again, I tried to deny my feelings. It wasn't normal. Well, not for me, anyway. *I'm gonna have to hand in my notice. But that will mean that I won't see Sam anymore.* Just the thought turned my stomach into a ball of screwed-up barbed wire. *And what about Katie? I can't do this to her. She will be disgusted. If I'm going to take this any further, I must do the honourable thing. It's not like we're married or anything.* I decided to talk to her that evening.

But things didn't go as planned.

Sam called us together in the middle of the workshop.

"Good news. We've secured a huge contract to service JP Hire Company's fleet of rental cars. They are the biggest car hire company in this county. It means we'll be able to expand. I'm opening another garage in the next county in two months' time."

Everyone cheered, clapped and whistled. Sam held up a hand. "So, to thank you all for your hard work and continuing support, I've arranged a little celebration at the pub. The beers are on me!"

Several drinks later, their effect giving me false confidence, I made my way towards Sam. "Can I...buy you a... celebration...a...umm... celebratory drink?"

"I'm sorry, Graham, I've got to get going. I promised to see my grandmother this evening, she's

119

cooking me dinner."

My heart beat faster. My face burned. "Okay! No problem!" I turned and strode towards the Gents. I stood looking into the mirror for ages. I had rings under my eyes and I was looking gaunt. I closed my eyes and took some deep breaths. When I felt more composed, I splashed water on to my face and made my way back to the bar. But Sam had gone.

I stayed in the pub longer than I should. The others had left about an hour earlier. Katie would be upset. I hadn't even phoned to say I'd be late. I needn't have worried, though; she wasn't there when I got back. She'd left a note on the kitchen table. *I've been trying to reach you on your mobile, but it's switched off. I expect you've forgotten I'm starting my new course this evening. Your dinner is in the oven. See you about 10.30.*

She wasn't even angry. Tears pricked the back of my eyes. Lovely Katie. She had always supported me and had encouraged me to apply for this job. She said it could lead to moving up to manager someday. I fell back on to the sofa. *What am I doing with my life? I'm going to ruin everything.*

I jumped up and walked round and round the room, playing all the possible scenarios in my head. At one point, I even noticed I had one hand clenched into a fist and was rubbing the other with it. *What did that mean?* Sighing, I sat down again. *I'm going to resign.* I had to. I couldn't go on like this. I was making a fool of myself and I'd end up with nothing.

The next morning, I went to work with a hastily scribbled letter of resignation in my pocket and waited for Sam to arrive. However, I became engrossed in a tricky oil change and missed my opportunity.

Just before lunch, Sam called me to the office. Again, my face was burning as I closed the door behind me. Looking into those blue eyes, I reached into my pocket for the letter. Sam touched my hand to stop me. A electric shock ran through my body. Sweating, I looked away.

"Graham, I know what's going on here. I know what you'd like to happen but it can't. It won't! There's someone else, you see."

"I... thought you... felt the same." Fidgeting, I carried on. "I've got it all so wrong." I looked away, rubbing the back of my neck. "God! Oh God, I am so... sorry. I've ... Look! I'll go... leave... now." My shoulders dropped and I had a fleeting image of *Paint Your Wagon*, when Lee Marvin asks the ground to swallow him up. I wished I were there now.

"Look, Graham, I have a proposition for you. I don't want to lose you, you're a good worker. I need someone to manage the new garage I mentioned yesterday. How would you feel about taking that on? It would put some distance between us."

Looking out of the window, I replied, "Can I think about it?"

"Well, yes. But I need your answer soon as I'll need to advertise. Can you get back to me by the end of the week?"

I went home that evening with a thumping headache. Katie was out at her course again. I sighed in annoyance. *I thought it was once a week, not every bloody night!* Although, in a way, I was glad she wasn't there. As was usual these days, I picked at the dinner she'd left me, throwing most of it into the bin.

I felt sick. I thought Sam felt the same way about me. How could I have misinterpreted the signals – or did I? Was this just a ruse? I had to give it one last shot. If that didn't work, I would take the job and move on. Maybe Katie would like a change of scenery.

I knew Sam often worked late, so I thought I'd go to the factory, see if the lights were on and maybe, when it was a bit quieter, talk the situation through. As I walked to the garage, I tried to compose myself. I practised a little speech, muttering as I walked, explaining my feelings, asking whether there was any chance at all that we could be together. Make clear my willingness to keep things quiet for the sake of the business and other workers.

The lights were on. Good. I unlocked the door and let myself in. Mechanics had their own sets of keys. Once I'd closed the door, I heard voices coming from Sam's office.

Damn! I can't go in now. I turned to leave but as I reached the exit, I heard Sam's voice coming from the office. I ducked behind one of the cars. Sam switched off the office light and turned on the stairwell light.

Sam carried on talking. "Once he goes to the other office, it'll keep him busy and we'll have a bit more time together."

I couldn't see who Sam was talking to, but by the way she was looking, it must have been the someone else she'd told me about.

As they came down the stairs, Katie said, "I'm so excited, we'll be together at last."

Secrets and Lies

by Kim Grove

Jenny was seated at her counter. She was supposed to be doing the next day's order. Instead, she was running through a field of barley that sparkled in the mid-day sun. Her blond wavy hair fanned out behind her, arms outstretched, her gipsy skirt billowing as she ran towards the man of her dreams. His face faded in and out, but she could see the short dark hair, the cornflower blue eyes and his muscles rippling beneath the tight shirt, sleeves rolled up to display his biceps.

She watched, as if she were on TV, but as she did so, her legs became tangled in her skirt, causing her to falter. Thorns ripped at her ankles and her cheeks became flushed with the heat of the day. The man faded completely as the shop-door bell alerted her to a customer.

"Morning, Mrs Johnson," Jenny got up from the chair. "How's Carol?"

"Morning, Jenny. She's feeling very sore and rather sorry for herself. I thought I'd take her some flowers to cheer her up." She handed over a bunch of daffodils and some white freesias she'd picked up from the display buckets outside the shop.

As Jenny wrapped them, the bell rang again. Jenny gasped silently at the man who walked in. Apart from the lack of a tight shirt, he was the man from her daydream.

"I'll be with you in just a moment, sir," she said her cheeks burning.

"How much do I owe you?" asked Mrs Johnson, who turned towards the man and smiled. Turning back to Jenny, she raised her eyebrows.

"Call it five pounds, and give Carol my love."

"Will do," Mrs Johnson said as she left, looking backwards and forwards between Jenny and the man.

Jenny turned to her new customer. "Can I help you?"

"I've come to pick up the flowers I ordered earlier. Stephens, Dan Stephens."

"Oh yes, you said to put anything into the bouquet, so I've put together a lovely bunch of wild flowers." Jenny smiled as she showed him the bouquet she'd retrieved from a bucket behind the counter. "They're my favourites."

"Wow, they're beautiful," he said smiling at her. Jenny pictured a halo of sunrays surrounding him. "I hope my date likes them."

"Well, if she doesn't, you know someone who does," she laughed as she wrapped the flowers, then checked herself. "That's if it is a 'she' of course." She dropped her eyes quickly and her cheeks reddened.

He smiled at her and the sparkle in his eyes caused her heart to flutter. The doorbell rang again and in skipped two young girls, talking at once, followed by a harassed woman.

"Can I see the flowers?"

"What does my posy look like?"

"How much do I owe you?" Mr Stephens said looking Jenny directly in the eye and smiling.

"That's thirty-seven pounds, please."

He opened his wallet, and went to take out a card,

but changed his mind and offered her two twenty pound notes instead.

Jenny frowned, but beamed at him as he looked up.

"And I hope you have a lovely evening," she said as she handed over the change.

"I doubt it," Jenny heard him mutter as he left the shop.

"Now, let's get you your flowers," she said to the girls.

* * * * *

Later, that evening, Jenny was sitting relaxing on the sofa at her friends' house. Alan and Marcia had invited her round for dinner, but Alan had not arrived home yet.

"Alan will be a bit late, I'm afraid. What can I get you to drink?"

"Don't be afraid, it's ages since we've had a chat, just the two of us. And a glass of wine would be lovely."

Marcia went into the kitchen to open the wine, returning with a large glass. She offered it to Jenny then joined her on the couch. Jenny smelt the waft of her perfume as she sat, Chanel Allure, she knew. She'd bought it for Marcia for her last birthday. It was her favourite and it suited her. It was quite a sophisticated perfume, and Marcia was a sophisticated woman, and very bright. Long dark shiny hair, large brown, kohl ringed eyes, and always smart in her well cut skirt suits as she attended university to teach future linguists several of the five languages she spoke fluently.

"What's that you're drinking?" Jenny nodded at

her friend's glass.

"Lemonade."

"Lemonade!"

"I'm saving myself for dinner."

Jenny squinted at her. "Have you got something to tell me? You're not expecting again, are you?"

Marcia smirked and shook her head. "No! I have three lovely children. I don't think there will be any more." She went silent and sat looking at her lap.

"Marcia, what's wrong?"

Marcia opened her mouth to say something, but shut it again as the front door opened.

Jenny frowned and looked at her friend, who shook her head slightly as Alan came in to the lounge.

"How are my two favourite girls?" he said, bounding towards each of them in turn, kissing them on the cheek. "Sorry I'm late, darling. There was a terrible mix up with the orders at work; the new computer system. I didn't think I would make it at all. Drinks?"

They declined. Alan went into the kitchen to get his own drink, then came and sat on the sofa opposite them.

"Alan, what's that you're drinking? Not you as well. I seem to be drinking alone tonight?"

"Oh, it's water, I had a bacon sandwich earlier and it's made me thirsty. Don't worry, I'll soon catch you up."

"Anyway," Marcia said, looking at Jenny. "How are you getting on finding the man of your dreams?"

"Oh, Marcia! I don't have time for that. I'm far too busy with the shop. And you know blokes always dump me after a couple of weeks."

"For goodness sake, Jenny, are you going to stay alone for the rest of your life? Not all men are like

126

Paul. I thought that after you divorced him, you'd be inundated with offers. I can see I'm going to have to help you to find that that elusive man." Marcia raised her eyebrows and looked Jenny directly in the eye. It was a look Jenny understood and one that Alan didn't see.

"Well, I'll be glad of the help. Just make sure he's extremely nice and really good-looking. And doesn't want to hop into bed with everyone else!"

"I'll do my best," Marcia smiled and Jenny nodded back, giving her a slight wink as Marcia's phone vibrated on the coffee-table. She reached for it and looked at the face, mouthing the words 'Stella' at Jenny as she got up and went in to the kitchen.

Jenny was alone with Alan and she was comfortable with this, although she knew Marcia wouldn't be. So when he came to sit next to her, she got up and retrieved her handbag, feigning the need for a tissue, then sat on the pouffe.

She looked at his short, dirty-blond hair and faded blue eyes. They gave him a laid-back aura he'd had since school where they had been great friends; well, a little more than that.

"How's business?" she finally asked.

"It's going really well, actually. We're in the middle of an expansion programme. We've got a huge contract from China."

"Wow! That's great."

"Yes. We're updating all our systems. Stock control, ordering, transport. Our old systems were too slow and not fit for purpose. I put the work out to tender and some chap I knew from Uni put in a bid, a good one too. He's done really well for himself since leaving. His IT business is one of the biggest in the country. So he got the job."

Marcia dashed back in to the lounge.

"Oh Jenny, I'm so sorry." She looked flustered. "That was Stella. Her car has broken down and she was just about to leave for the airport. We gonna have to go round, see if Alan can get the car started quickly. If not, we'll have to take them to the airport. Can you look after the kids while we go and sort them out?"

"Of course I can. Go on, both of you. Don't worry about me."

"I'm so sorry, Jen. I think we'll be gone a while. I don't think we'll be back 'til late. I was really looking forward to this evening."

Jenny walked into the hallway with them and watched as Marcia grabbed her jacket from the coat rack and her handbag from the hall cupboard.

"Come on, Alan." Marcia looked in rather a hurry to leave. "Let's go, or they'll miss their flight!"

Jenny stood at the door to see them off. As Marcia got to the car she called out, "Don't let the food go to waste. Starters and desserts are in the fridge and the hotpot is in the oven. It'll be ready in an hour."

"I'll be fine," Jenny called and waved her away. "Give my love to Stella and the girls."

Jenny wandered back into the lounge and flopped down on to the sofa. What a great evening this is going to be, she thought. Alone again! She got up. She loved Marcia's house, it was so homely. Three large sofas, as soft as a heap of cotton wool, were set facing a wood-burning stove. Soft furnishings in hues of cream and brown, so expertly combined, made it warm and cosy.

She wandered into the dining-room and stood looking at the table Marcia had set. It was lovely. Plain white crockery and table linen blended perfectly with the silver cutlery and a posy of pale pink roses that Marcia had asked her to bring.

She had obviously gone to a lot of trouble. But something wasn't quite right. As Jenny stood staring at the table, frowning, a bump from upstairs made her jump.

She climbed the stairs and looked into the girls' room, they were both asleep. The sight of them gently breathing made her sigh, they looked so peaceful. Lily was tangled up in her Peppa Pig duvet. Jenny went over and straightened it out. Scarlett's animal sticker book lay open beside her. Jenny picked it up, closed it, put it on to the bedside table, and pulled the duvet over the child's bare arms.

She went into Luke's room, he was asleep too, but a wooden train had slipped off his bed. She picked it up, put it on top of the toy-box, crept out of his room, and quietly closed the door.

As she walked across the landing, the doorbell rang. She cringed, afraid the children would wake.

"Oh no, what have they forgotten?"

She opened the door and stared open-mouthed.

"Jenny? Hello!" the dreamy chap from her shop said, offering her the bouquet of flowers she had arranged for him earlier.

It was then that she realised what was bothering her about the dining-table. It was set for two.

* * * * *

Jenny was watching the TV when she heard the front door open.

"Did your sister get her flight on time?" she said, smirking.

"Yes, thank goodness," Marcia said. "They

haven't had a holiday for a couple of years now, and they were really looking forward to it." She ran upstairs.

"I'm starving," Alan cut in. "I hope you've left me some hotpot, Jen."

"Oh. Ha! Ha!"

"What d'you mean by that?"

"As if you don't know!"

Jenny looked at Alan for a few seconds.

"What?"

"It's okay. I don't mind. He was nice. You didn't have to go out; a foursome would have been alright."

"What are you two talking about?" Marcia had come back in to the room.

"Well, I have no idea what Jenny is talking about," Alan said.

"Oh stop it, the pair of you."

"Jenny, I really don't know what you're talking about." His brow wrinkled, and Alan ran his fingers through his hair. "What's happened?"

"Dan's what happened. You arranged for Dan to come and have dinner with me. A blind date!"

"What?" Marcia and Alan cried.

"Look, you can stop pretending now. We got on so well, we're going to see each other again." She smiled at each of them.

Alan got up, and went to kneel in front of Jenny. He took Jenny's hand in his, but she pulled away. "Jenny," he said quietly. "I promise you, we didn't arrange for anyone to come round. I don't know anyone called Dan. Do you, Marcia?"

"No, I don't." Marcia said rubbing her neck in concern but Jenny could see a look of hope in her eyes.

"But you must have," Jenny's eyes widened and

she stared at her friends in turn.

Marcia shook her head. "What happened, Jenny?"

Jenny told them about the flowers in the shop... Alan and Marcia not drinking... leaving her in a rush... the table set for two.

At that point, Marcia cut in. "Oh God! Alan originally said he wouldn't be home in time, so I set the table for the two of us. I can see why you thought we had set this up."

Jenny told them she and Dan had a lot in common. They liked the same books, went to the same restaurants, had seen the same films. He had his own business like her, and they laughed. They laughed a lot.

Jenny sighed, "He was perfect. Well, perhaps not perfect, but certainly getting there."

"But, what explanation did he give about coming here tonight?" Marcia said.

Jenny sat for a moment trying to remember what was said during the evening. "I don't think he did. I think I just assumed, because of the table and the way you rushed out, that it was a blind date, so I didn't question it."

"And you're seeing him again?" she said.

"Yes, on Sunday. I'm going to watch him play football."

"I don't like it, Jenny," Alan said. "He could be anyone. How did he know you were here? How did he know we'd go out? I'm really worried about this. He came into our home uninvited. He could have been a murderer. Or worse!"

"But he seemed really nice." Jenny's shoulders drooped and she stared down at her hands, then she said quietly, "I really liked him."

"Look," Marcia said. "Why don't we come with

you to the football match? Let us check him out; ask him a few questions, like how he knew you'd be here by yourself."

"I'd be much happier about you seeing him then, Jen," Alan said. "I know it sounds like we're being mean, but I really don't want anything awful to happen to you. I wouldn't forgive myself."

"Okay. I'm sure he won't mind. If he really cares." Jenny looked at her friends. "You're so good to me you two. You're like guardian angels."

"Well, let's hope we're not dealing with the devil," Alan said.

"I'm sorry," Jenny said.

"What for?" Marcia said.

"There's not much hotpot left, I'm afraid. We ate most of it. But we did have a lovely meal, thanks to you, Marcia," she said laughing.

* * * * *

Sunday arrived. Jenny had texted Dan during the week to confirm the details and to tell him Alan and Marcia were coming. He seemed quite happy about it.

The three of them sat on a bench along the touchline and waited for play to start. The players ran on to the pitch and Jenny craned her neck. "Oh!" she said. "He's not there."

"Maybe he's a substitute," Marcia suggested.

Jenny half-stood to get a better view of the substitutes, who were sitting on a bench along the touchline from them. "I can't see him! He's not there!" She turned towards Alan and Marcia, her shoulders slumped and she sighed. "He's not coming, is he?"

"There's bound to be a reason," Marcia said.

"Yes," Alan started, grabbing Jenny's hand. "There's probably a simple explanation."

Jenny pulled her hand away, grabbed her handbag from under the bench and rummaged around for a tissue to dab her eyes, when she noticed her mobile phone. She took it out, dropping her bag on to the ground. On the opening screen was a text message from Dan. It said, "Sorry, can't make football. Have to work. Will ring later."

"Oohh," Jenny said giving them both a teary-eyed smile. "He's had to work, he can't make it." She watched Alan look at Marcia.

"What?"

"Are you sure he was going to come today?" Alan said.

"Of course, here's his message." She turned her phone round for him to see.

He glanced at it and shrugged his shoulders. "Anyone could have sent that," he said quietly. "And I'm not staying here to watch this lot play football. I should have been at work. We've got more problems with our new IT system."

"I didn't ask you to come!"

"I know, but I'm worried about you, Jen. We don't know this bloke from Adam. I don't even know whether he actually exists."

"What are you saying? Don't you believe me? You think I'm making this up?"

"Are you?" Alan murmured.

"God!" Jenny jumped up, grabbed her handbag and marched towards the park exit.

"She's not a child, Alan," she heard Marcia say as she left.

* * * * *

Instead of going home, Jenny stopped at Ben's Wine Bar.

"Hi, Ben," she said to the barman.

"Jenny! Hi, how are you? How's business?"

"It's going well, actually. Better than I thought it would."

"What can I get you?"

"I think I'll have a large glass of red, please."

"On your own?"

"Yes! Again!" She gave him a weak smile.

As he smiled back, she could feel tears prick the back of her eyes again. She fiddled in her handbag for her purse and then played with the change until he returned with her wine. She handed over the money then took herself far away from him, settling into an armchair by the window.

As she dropped her bag on to the floor beside her, she heard the familiar tone of a text. "Where are you?" it said.

"In Ben's Wine Bar."

"On your own?"

"Yes!"

"Finished my work. Can I join you?"

Her heart beat faster. What should she say? She knew Alan and Marcia were worried about her. Still, if she stayed here, Ben was about. She was sure he would help her if she got into any difficulties.

"That would be great."

He didn't take long to get there.

"Hi," he said when he arrived, kissing her on the cheek. "I went to the ground, but couldn't see you there."

"Well, there wasn't much point in staying if you weren't there, was there?"

"I suppose not."

* * * * *

In the shop the next morning, the doorbell brought Jenny back to the present with a bump. She'd been thinking about yesterday and the warm cosy feeling she had disappeared the moment she saw Alan standing in the entrance.

"Hi, Jen," he said striding towards her. He came around the counter and hugged her, pinning her arms to her side, rocking her backwards and forwards, kissing her on her forehead, on her cheek, then very faintly brushing her lips with his.

"Get off!" She twisted free of his embrace, and pushed him away, frowning. "What's wrong with you?"

"What?"

"I know what you're doing. You're so transparent, but it's not going to happen, Alan. I will not hurt Marcia. You and I finished a long time ago. Permanently! Nothing is going to happen between us, so you might as well get all thoughts of that, out of your mind. Now! What are you doing here, anyway?"

"I came to say I'm sorry. I am sorry," Alan said, head bowed. He looked like a small child who had been told off.

"I don't think we should see so much of each other anymore."

"Oh come on, Jenny! Don't be daft." He raised his hands as if to plead with her.

"Daft! You called me a liar! You think I'm making Dan up! Well, I've got news for you! Dan met me after the match yesterday and took me to dinner. He paid for everything. He was a total gentleman. Unlike someone I know! All you do these days is leer at me; paw me like I'm your mate! In front of Marcia as well! That's unforgivable."

Alan looked at her for what seemed like an age. She was just about to turn away, when he shook his head and sighed. "Okay, Jen. I hear you and I'm sorry. I truly am. I don't want us to fall out. You're my one true friend. I'd still like to meet this Dan, though. It would make me feel better. What about the four of us going out for dinner?"

Jenny burst into tears.

"Jenny!" Alan said, hugging her to him. This time she didn't pull away. "What's the matter?" He waited for an answer but none came. So he continued, "Jenny, I'm worried about you. I'm worried that he's been stalking you. That he's up to no good. If I could meet him, it would put my mind at rest. That's all I want to do. We've always been good friends, even after you dumped me! But, I don't want to ruin that now. I just want to make sure you're safe. You can understand that, can't you?"

"I suppose so," Jenny said pulling away and wiping her eyes with the back of her hand.

"Here!" Alan handed her a handkerchief from his pocket.

She dried her eyes, blew her nose on it, then offered it to him. "D'you want it back?" she giggled, then nodded, "I'll talk to Dan."

* * * * *

The following day, Jenny received a text from Marcia saying, "Can we meet?"

They met at lunchtime in Ben's Wine Bar. Marcia could only spare a couple of minutes, as she had to get back for a lecture.

Marcia came to the point as she sat and took a sip

of her lemonade. "Alan has been really distracted ever since your divorce and I'm worried about him. How was he yesterday?"

"What do you mean?"

"Did he try anything on?"

"You needn't worry, Marcia... "

"Look, I know you two were together before you both went to Uni…"

"Honestly, Marcia. There's nothing to worry about on my part."

Jenny saw the tears well in Marcia's eyes.

"Marcia, please. You have to believe me."

Marcia pulled a tissue out of her handbag, and dabbed at her eyes, trying not to dislodge her make-up. "I hope you can cope with his advances, I know he'll try it on with you."

"Look, Marcia, nothing's going to happen between us. I promise."

"He can be very persuasive."

Jenny looked at her friend, pursing her lips, wondering whether to tell her or not. Taking a big sigh, she made her decision. "Marcia, I'm going to tell you something. But, you must promise me that you won't say anything about our conversation to Alan or anyone else for that matter. And I want you to do something for me in return."

As Jenny talked, Marcia's mouth opened and her eyes widened, but when she finished, Jenny saw her light up, as if the sun had finally come out from behind a black cloud. Marcia reached over and gave Jenny a hug, holding on for a few seconds, as if saying a silent thank you. Then Marcia rushed from Ben's Wine Bar as her calendar alerted her of the time to leave.

* * * * *

It was two weeks before they could put their plan into action. It hadn't been easy for Marcia to arrange. But, when Dan and Jenny arrived at the restaurant, Marcia was sitting alone at a table, waiting for them.

"You managed it then?"

Marcia nodded, smiling at the two of them. "And you must be Dan. It's lovely to meet you at long last." Jenny watched Marcia shake Dan's hand.

Dan looked her up and down, beaming. "Jenny didn't tell me you were so beautiful."

"Oh, stop it," Marcia smiled looking down, clearly pleased with the compliment.

Jenny had to fight to keep the smile on her face. "Shall we sit?" she said.

They got on well together, laughing, drinking and eating. It's nice to see Marcia looking so relaxed and comfortable, Jenny thought, although she was a bit worried at one point when Marcia asked Dan, "How did you come to be at our house that first evening?"

Jenny watched Dan answer the question with ease. "Well. After I saw Jenny in her shop, I was so taken with her, I gave up on my blind date for that evening. Instead, and I'm sorry to admit this, I waited for her to finish work and I followed her." He held his hands up as if to submit and gave her a coy smile. "She ended up at your house. I watched her go in and was going to wait for her, catch her on the way out. Give her the flowers and confess my undying love for her."

At this point, he laughed, took hold of Jenny's hand, gave it a squeeze and smiled at her.

He continued, "But you went out, so I assumed that she was babysitting for you and I thought I'd take a chance. I was just going to say hello and leave, but she invited me in and to have dinner with her. I couldn't believe my luck! She seemed to think I was her blind date, and explained where she thought you had gone, and I knew you would be coming back fairly early, so I thought it best not to hang around."

"I thought it would be something like that," Marcia said. "Well, good for you! She's a lovely girl, as you can see, and a great friend. My husband, Alan, has been rather worried about her. He's known her since they were at school and they're very close. We didn't want anything bad to happen to her."

"Yes, she told me," he said, glancing at Jenny.

Jenny was conscious of Dan watching them as they chatted away. Every now and again, she would look at him and catch him gazing at Marcia, frowning. At one point, Jenny grabbed his hand under the table and gave it a squeeze. He squeezed it back and beamed at her.

At the end of the meal, Dan asked for the bill, paying this while Jenny and Marcia visited the Ladies.

"What do you think?" Jenny asked.

"He's lovely, Jenny. I can see why you like him. We'll keep Alan away, give you a chance to get to know him."

They left the restaurant together. After seeing Marcia safely to her car, Dan held his car door open for Jenny. He got in and sat at the wheel, not moving.

"Is everything OK, Dan?" Jenny said. "Did I say something wrong? Did Marcia say something wrong?"

Dan didn't move.

"Please, Dan…what is it?"

Silhouetted against the darkness, Jenny saw Dan turn towards her.

"There's something I need to tell you," he said softly.

Jenny's heart thumped for the entire ten minutes it took to drive back to her house. It started to rain. The night was bleak.

They ran up the garden path, sheltering in the porch whilst Jenny rummaged around her handbag for the key.

Once inside, Jenny let Dan lead her to the sofa, where he sat, pulling her to sit next to him. He explained what was bothering him. There were tears, raised voices, accusations and finally acceptance. He left four hours later.

Jenny watched Dan from her bedroom window as he walked to his car. He turned and looked directly at her. She lifted her hand and gave a half-wave, but he had already turned away.

"Goodbye, Dan," she whispered.

* * * * *

Jenny met Marcia from work the next evening. They went into Ben's Wine Bar, ordered a glass of wine each and took themselves to sofa at the rear.

"You were right about Alan," Jenny said.

Marcia looked at her, "What do you mean?"

Jenny took a deep breath and told Marcia what had happened. They spent the rest of the evening discussing what they should do about it.

* * * * *

A year flew past. Jenny had continued to meet Marcia every week at Ben's Wine Bar, her business went from strength to strength, thanks to her improved use of social media, and she'd had so little spare time, she'd hardly seen Alan.

Marcia remarked on how well Jenny looked. She approved of Jenny's new hairstyle and said her eyes sparkled these days. They laughed a lot whenever they met.

But the day finally came when Jenny knew things would change.

She threw the curtains open and looked out on to a sunny early September day. A heat wave had been promised and she was glad. The outfit she'd chosen would be perfect.

The knock at the door came three hours before she was due to leave. She knew he'd leave it that late. Her front door opened straight on to the living room, and she could tell by the silhouette it was him. Although she was in her dressing-gown, she took a deep breath and opened the door.

"Alan," she whispered and stood back to let him in.

He pushed past. "What the bloody hell's this?" he said throwing a small card at her face. She watched it flutter to the floor, leaving it where it landed.

"You can see what it is."

"You've been seeing someone behind my back!"

Jenny raised her eyebrows at him. "What? I need your permission now, do I?"

He dragged his fingers through his hair and turned away from her, pacing the room. "It's got today's date on it!" he yelled, flinging his arm at the card. "How did you know we could make it?"

"Marcia knew all about it. You can't blame us, can you?"

"You never mentioned you were seeing someone else."

"Of course I didn't. Why would I?"

"Because… because…you should!"

"Why? So you can warn him off again?"

"What the bloody hell are you talking about?"

"Because that's what you do! That's what you've always done, isn't it?" she said, eyes narrowing, arms crossed.

"I don't know what you're talking about!"

"Alan," she said, "I know everything."

"You know nothing! You're a liar and a cheat!"

"I know everything, Alan," she repeated quietly. "And so does Marcia."

"What the hell are you talking about?"

"You've warned off all my previous boyfriends. I know that you have a photograph of me on your desk. Marcia knows that too."

Jenny watched as Alan's face reddened and beads of sweat started to appear at his hairline. "I don't know what you're talking about."

"So you don't have a photo of me on your desk?"

"No! Yes! How would you know that?" he paused. "Wait a minute," he picked the card up and looked at it. "Steven! Steven bloody Daniels! You've been seeing Steve Daniels?"

"Yes, and he told me everything. You warned him not to see me, didn't you?"

"He's stolen you from me," he yelled, jabbing his finger towards her.

"I'm not yours to steal, actually. You're married, for goodness sake! Marcia's my friend and a wonderful person. What do you think she'd say if she heard you talking like this?"

"Leave her out of this!"

"Why? This involves her too," Jenny said.

"So, how did you two meet?"

"He turned up on your doorstep," she replied.

"What?"

"He turned up on your doorstep. He said he was Dan Stephens and he had followed me there. You'd told him I was trying to find a new chap, but that you wanted to put me off, because you fancied your chances. You told him a bit too much, really. Like where I worked, for instance. He found me easily enough. It's a good job he wasn't a murderer, as you suggested! After he met Marcia, he was really angry with you. He thought she was so lovely, that you didn't deserve her. So when he took me home that night, he told me everything."

Jenny thought back to that night. It had been terrible and wonderful. She had refused to believe Alan had tried to stop her seeing anyone. She was angry with Steve for his deception. Then at Alan for his behaviour. She had cried a lot. But then, after Steve had explained how he felt and told her he wanted to be with her for the rest of his life, she had accepted everything. That was the first night they had made love.

Jenny watched for Alan's reaction. He had now paled and he combed his hands through his hair. However, the sweat was now pouring down his cheeks and he pulled up his t-shirt to dry his face. Jenny looked at the taut muscles of his abdomen. He still looked as good as he did when they were together.

"I thought, being the way you are, it was best not to say anything more to you, not to see you so often," Jenny sighed.

"What do you mean, with me 'being the way I am'?"

"I know how you feel about me, Alan. I'm not

143

stupid. The lingering hands, the wistful kisses."

"Oh, don't flatter yourself!"

"Why are you here, then?" she asked. "Nothing will ever happen between us. I'm not going to hurt Marcia. She's my best friend."

She looked at him and saw the change in him too late to react. He jumped at her, pinning her shoulders against the wall, and tried to kiss her on her lips. She moved her head to the side and he kissed her on the cheek instead.

"I love you, Jenny," he hissed. "You know I've always loved you."

"Get off," she gasped, and tried to push him away.

He ignored her and attempted to kiss her again. Panting he said, "I know you feel the same way."

"No, Alan. You don't understand. We can't be together."

Alan tried to kiss her again, but Jenny, writhing to try to free herself, said, "Alan, we can't be together. Not like that."

Jenny heard the faint click of the front door, and smelling Marcia's Chanel Allure, breathed a sigh of relief.

"We can't be together, I won't ever hurt Marcia."

"But, I love you, tell me you don't love me."

Jenny looked in to Alan's eyes, and saw an image of herself. "I do love you, Alan. But not in that way. I can't love you in that way."

"Why not?" he breathed kissing her neck.

"Because she's your sister," Marcia's voice cut in.

"What?" He spun round.

Jenny watched as his eyes widened and he looked backwards and forwards between them, his eyes pleading. "You're my brother," Jenny said quietly.

"I am not," he said, as he pulled his hands off her

shoulders.

"You are."

"No!"

"Yes!"

Alan flumped down on to the sofa, staring at the floor.

Jenny looked at Marcia and pulled a face at her, suggesting that she didn't know what to do next. She finally decided to sit down next to him. He deserved an explanation.

"After my dad first met you, he knew. He told me he'd had a brief fling with your mother."

She stopped, picturing the confrontation, then shook the image away from her mind and whispered, "I was so angry with him! So angry he hadn't told me. We were breaking the law, for Christ's sake! I felt sick. I didn't want to accept it! I really loved you, you know." She tipped her head looking up at his downturned face, and gave a fleeting smile, then continued. "But once I'd calmed down and looked closer at you I could see the resemblance between you and Dad. And me. That's why I finished with you. That's why I went away to university on the other side of the country. I needed to get over you. I needed you to get over me. I thought you had."

"I thought you'd found someone else," he muttered, tears starting to fall. "I was so jealous of anyone you even looked at. Why didn't you tell me?"

"My dad begged me not to. He said he'd made a promise to your mother that he would keep quiet, he didn't want anyone to think badly of your mum. And he didn't want my mum to find out, of course. I didn't agree with him, but I thought as I was going away to Uni…"

"I've always loved you, Jenny. If I'd have known

all this, I could have got on with my life. It's been so unfair on Marcia. I've been so unfair on Marcia." He looked up at his wife, "I'm so sorry, darling." His head dropped.

"Jenny told me all about this a while ago," she said softly. "That's why you haven't seen much of her over the last year. She needed time to get to know Steve. See whether, after Paul, she could trust him."

Jenny cut in. "I thought if I got married again, you would forget about me. That I wouldn't have to tell you. But… "

He sat, head bowed, his body shaking, his tears dampening the carpet beneath his feet. Marcia sat down next to him, reached for his hand and gave it a faint squeeze. He looked at her, gave her a watery smile and put his head on her shoulder. "I'm so sorry," he whispered. "I do love you, you know." He sniffed and tried to brush the tears away but they kept coming.

Jenny gave him a couple of minutes before saying, "Alan, I need you to do something for me."

"What?"

She knelt in front of him, took his hands in hers, then said gently, "I want you to give me away at my wedding."

He looked at her, his tears were starting to subside, but he shook his head.

"Please, Alan. You're all the family I have left."

He looked at her for a long time. "I don't know if I can," he uttered.

She looked at him, her eyes pleading. "Please, Alan." She looked at Marcia and gave a faint wink. "I'll understand if you won't. Marcia can give me away instead."

He gave a brief smile, head to one side. "That's a

bit cheeky, isn't it?"

She waited in silence, looking at him, watching his face for signs of acceptance.

"Okay." He waited before adding, "On one condition."

"What? Anything!"

"You change out of that dressing gown; I'm not giving you away in that!"

He took her hands in his and kissed them.

Liz Heywood

Liz Heywood has lived in the South Pacific for 35 years where she taught creative writing. She has now retired to Wellingborough in the UK with her husband and a house full of books. She publishes poetry, short stories, and novels under the name Beth Heywood. When Liz is not writing, she enjoys walking, reading, gardening, and sailing the seas on merchant ships.

Childhood Memories

by Liz Heywood

Sun burns bright across the pavement
    Precious toys are set aside
Insects humming in summer sunshine
    Suddenly I'm called inside

Away from games with friends and playmates
    Annexed fearful I'm thrust inside
Into the sitting- room, freshly polished
    There's no place here to run and hide

"Hello Dad, it's nice to see you
    Have I broken any rule?"
Stern-faced, unresponsive, you roll your sleeves up,
    And set your foot upon the stool

"I just don't know, I still don't get it
    Whatever can be the matter?
What's that you've got behind your back
    Hidden in the folds on your jacket?"

You've raised my dress, you've dropped my knickers
    Stop oh stop oh please
Not the cane, I hid the cane
    Wet warmth runs down my knees

I hope you're glad, I hope you're proud
    I can hear you panting loud
There's a lesson to be learned – MY love and respect
    For you, is yet to be learned.

Dreams of Happiness

by Liz Heywood

Four pairs of eyes intelligent excited,
    "We're going, Mum. We won't be back."
Airport throngs multitudes weeping,
    "It's all right Mum, DON'T CRY!"

Friends gather around my children
    Sharing young jokes I don't understand
Flights called, cuddles kisses, away they go,
    Cell phones are now switched off.

Cathay Pacific taxis first,
    Carrying my first-born and his bride to an
unknown land.
Asian eyes scrutinize me, alert for signs of weakness
    As they take away my boy.

Warm Maori arms enfold me
    The Pommie flight's going now
Taking someone's brown-eyed daughter,
    The wife of my blue-eyed son.

"He'll be back, you've got whanau,
    You're one of us now
Let's go to the pub – you'll soon feel better " 'Thanks
but
    How can I be better when both my boys are gone?"

Escape from Albania

by Liz Heywood

Streets ablaze, soldiers looting
    Panic in my mind
Clutching my jewellery and new-born baby
    My darling husband's left behind

Airport's closed, locals arrested
    Back to the embassy we go
This sanctuary of peace and safety
Now crackling and aglow

'Copter blades whirring, marines shooting
    Please God we'll be all right
The ambassador's awn, mown for cucumber
sandwiches
    Not the apocalypse that stormed in tonight

Desperate men brawling frightened women crying
    Take us with you please
To a better lie a safer life
    Help oh help us PLEASE

Lifeboat's heading for Brindisi
    Dipping and plunging through icy seas
Almost there bright lights safety
    Leaving our friends on bended knees

Government officials greet us in Rome
    Showers, meals, comfortable beds
We'll soon by Home. But we've left our dog, Mabel,
for pie filling,
    With our starving Albanian friends.

Greg

by Liz Heywood

If I could put my hand inside the glass
    Unpeel your picture from the frame
I'd pull you back from your mistakes
    To the bosom of our family again.

I'd hold you closer to my heart,
    Never again would I let you stray
'Til you learned the lessons you needed to know
    Before you went away.

If I could hold you to my breast again
    Comfort, love, and self-esteem would be yours
But innocent you walk, with good school grades
    Gold-digging women wait with open jaws.

If I could put my hand inside the glass
    Unpeel your picture from the frame
I'd pull you back from your mistakes
    To the bosom of our family again.

Hong Kong

by Liz Heywood

Black velvet hair soft ebony eyes
    Designer suits you dress for success
The road into your family is long and difficult
    If my son loves the girl he must persist

Once inside all doors are open
    It will be worth it in the end
In exotic cafes and sophisticated restaurants
    In a woollen two-piece I'm out of my depth

Your siblings say my son's handsome
    Don't you see further than this?
Your parents aren't quite ready to meet me
    What am I, poor white trash?

Five long years you lived on my farm
    I cared for you when you were ill
Nurtured your homesick spirit
    Causing you to lose face

Five happy years you dined at our table
    Slept on the warmth and comfort of our bed
I helped you with your visas and language
    An older woman, you helped yourself to my son

As the oriental gates close behind him,
    Locking him into your ways forever,
In my plush hotel I empty drawers and wardrobes,
    Unwelcomed, I return home.

From Second Wife

by Liz Heywood

The younger woman holds the perfumed parcel in her
hands.
It has come from overseas, from a sad time, well
remembered now forgiven.

As the outer wrapping comes away the perfume
grows stronger. Pervades the entire room with its
joyful fragrance.
Had it been a wine it would be named 'embracing'
rather than 'pert' or 'pithy'.
But it is more than that.
As the inner wrapping unfolds it becomes
wholesome, forgiving, respectful, loving.
An acknowledgement to her as the mother of his
irreplaceable children.
A rite of passage, a salute to her as the first, and
therefore most important wife.

I need to find myself

by Liz Heywood

Silk blouses trailing from cardboard boxes
    The canary singing joyfully in its cage
Theatre tickets spilling from upturned vases
    I need to find myself

'Were you really that unhappy?
    Wasn't I always by your side?
Didn't you have the house you so wanted?
    Don't your parents live in the flat beneath?'

I'm taking the CDs so carefully chosen,
    The paintings you made when you were bored
You've got the pine trees we planted together
    I need to find myself

'Didn't we ski in Aspen Colorado?
    View the paintings in the Louvre?
On camel back we plodded across the Sahara,
    To please and delight you, I've always strived!'

I need to go into the city
    To find out what life's really about
To see if I can make it without you
    I'll be back for Christmas – *I need to find myself*

'I've taken you to the corners of the earth,
    Loved you with candles around the bath,
In a bedroom decked with flowers,
    Is it a baby? Tell me what you want'

155

No not a baby, something undefinable
  I need to find myself
You're given me everything – it isn*'t enough*
  I need to find myself.

'Over twenty years I've mortgaged my soul for you,
  It wasn't enough – I see that now – READY AIM
FIRE!
Now we've both found you, splattered on the walls
and the ceiling
  I've found yourself for you.'

Marking time

by Liz Heywood

Floral sheets, sunlit room, books, TV
 Life inside ain't too bad
Three meals a day, ironed corporate wardrobe
 Helps keep low self-esteem at bay.

Weekly visits from the hairdresser,
 Open prison ain't too bad
Visits from dentists, beauticians, gynaecologists,
 Prepare for release, that far away day

Ten-pin bowling teaches team work
 Working in groups ain't too bad
Growing vegetables, tending fruit trees
 Teaching how to live when we move away

Did I do it? Did I? Did I? The padre asks
 His face so sad
That's my secret, I'll tell no-one that I dream
 I blew my family away.

Ruth

by Liz Heywood

Your hair shines like the rays of sunshine
 Your smile lights up our days
Kindness emanates from your fingertips
 Our beloved golden child

We long for you and your dark-haired sisters
 Prepare a home with love and care
Your sisters come first, they find life difficult
 Then you arrive bringing happiness and laughter
Our beloved golden child

Always the peace-maker, never angry or difficult
 You organize and enrich all our lives
Mending broken animals and healing all our souls
 Do you know how much we admire and love you
 Our beloved, golden child?

After long hours sewing ball-gowns for your sisters
 You take your books into the sunshine
To study for your own career
 Our beloved golden child

What of your own life, Ruth? You're popular and
loved
 But there must be something that you need
Tell us, we'll get it for you – you've brought us so
much joy and happiness
 Our beloved golden child

Laughing and giggling you prepare for your own ball
    Life is going to be so good for you
Flushed and happy you return home early, 'I'm going
to be a Doctor, Mum, I've got to study'
    We're so proud of you, our beloved golden child

Dark-circled eyes, your hair lacks lustre,
    Take a year off, stay at home, where we can all
care for you
Our beloved golden child

You won't sleep you'll take no respite
    You are successful in the end
Graduating *summa cum laude*, we're so very proud of
you,
    Our beloved golden child.

You don't acknowledge our letters nor return our
phone calls,
    Our fears have driven us wild
In the end we break the door down
    Our beloved golden child

Stiff limbs cyanosed lips,
    We could see you were already dead
A wonderful sister a remarkable daughter
    You were sprawled half in half out of your bed.
We wept, and will always weep torrents,
    Our beloved golden child

Dead by your own hand. Didn't you know how much
we all loved you?
    Couldn't you have said, 'Mum, life's just too
hard?'

What was it that you couldn't handle? We'll never know now

Rest in peace, we'll always love you

Our cherished beloved golden child.

The Wind

by Liz Heywood

In ways too numerous to be counted,
    She slipped into our lives, quicksilver feet across
the grasses
Whispering, gentle, firm, bending all to her will,
    She breathes through the photos of our lives,
baskets of joy
Platters of optimism displayed on high for all to view.

Most times she storms in, times when we love her
best,
    With her salt from the ocean as she roars through
Pines, even the birds claw tightly to their branches,
she turns, coming
    From the south, opens our doors, screams through
our house.

Her fury tears paint from the walls, we pray to keep
her
    Out, as she shrieks round the eaves, rattles
windows
In their casings, demanding admittance. Will we
allow her
    To tear our lives apart?

At the base of the cliffs and hollows she whips the
surf in a fury.
    Again and again she pistol-whips the dunes
Trying to scream us out of our house. If we stay she'll
    Erode the cliffs beneath us and

We'll tumble like jetsam into the vortex, and screaming
   Will become part of her.

Making an English Lady

by Liz Heywood

Juliana, of the Clan MacDonald, was tied to a chair. Her body ached. Her heart ached. Her mind demanded to scream out the injustice of her short life. But it was useless. She was tightly gagged. Her heart thudded. She was captive. She was afraid.

Her eyes took in her opulent prison in the castle of Redbeard the Warrior.

At least this place was clean, and the logs, crackling and fizzing in the cavernous fireplace kept the large room pleasantly warm.

Things could have been worse.

Juliana couldn't scream. And if she could, it would have made no difference as her voice would have been muffled by the rich tapestries hanging from the thick stone walls of the bedchamber. For now, escape was out of the question. She would bide her time and seize her chance when it arose, as it surely would. After all, her captors were only Englishmen and therefore of limited intelligence and sophistication.

Her small bare feet were firmly secured to the chair-legs. She wiggled her toes on the thick sheepskin rugs that covered the large expanse of floor and led up to the steps of the dais to the massive four-poster bed that sat atop.

Thick velvet curtains, hanging from the top of the four-poster, were tied back to the bedposts by large tasseled cord. A silk sheet, strewn with large cushions, was arranged around its edges.

On the far side of the fireplace stood a large table, thick ebony legs supporting a brass top, inlaid with amethysts and rubies, probably a spoil of war. In the centre was a large carafe of wine, six silver goblets and a silver tray, holding bunches of black grapes and plump green olives.

This was a much pleasanter room than the dingy rush-strewn floors and narrow beds that she was used to in her native Scotland.

But most enchanting of all was the smell of fresh herbs that pervaded the air, as the room basked in the pink light a northern sunset can bring.

Indeed, things could have been far, far worse.

Juliana squirmed on her chair. The rough lines of her blouse chafed against her high breasts, bringing them to small tight peaks.

Tonight should have been her wedding night. The night for which she'd kept her young body pure. The night she should be sharing with her childhood sweetheart Duncan, the fresh-faced shepherd boy.

Instead, she was on a real adventure.

In her heart of hearts, Juliana had always yearned for more than she could have in a backward Scottish village.

And now she had it.

A twinge of guilt lapped her shoulders. She shrugged it away. Live hard, die young, life was too short for regrets.

She'd yearned for this night for long months, lying awake at night, her untouched body restless, sweating, anticipating the sweet transition from girl to

164

woman, only to have it snatched from her by the pagan English who knew nothing of the ways of the more couth Scots.

Last night, as the mists had swirled across the purple heather, the tow-headed English had struck. Only a handful of them, but they were strong and fearsome, their speed and silence taking sleeping clansmen by surprise. And in the rosy dawn, they'd galloped back out of the village, taking Juliana captive, bound helplessly, and carried on horseback far away from home to Castle Greystone, the home of Redbeard the Warrior.

If she could somehow manage to escape, she could return home with her reputation intact and still marry Duncan. She would at least have seen something of the world.

With a resounding crash, the heavy oak door to the chamber burst open, and Juliana gasped.

Silhouetted against the dusk stood Redbeard.

With broad shoulders and muscular hips, his body filled the entire doorway. He was a mountain of a man, and Juliana was shocked, for he was as strong and virile a specimen as she could ever hope to meet. And she was now his prize!

He strode into the room, closely flanked by two soldiers, one young and fair, the other older, darker. Redbeard was handsome, his soldiers menacing. As a trio, they were lethal.

For the first time in the young life, Juliana was unsure of herself.

Striding up to her, the younger English soldier roughly cut off her gag.

"My, but she's a pretty wench, lord."

"We'll have some fun with this one, for sure," said the other soldier, then to Juliana, "On your knees before your master!" He laughed. "Have you no manners?"

"I'm a Scot. I go on my knees for no-one!"

"You'll be on your back before the master's finished with you," snarled the younger soldier.

Redbeard silenced his men with a glance.

"Forgive them." His blue eyes flashed. "They're Border men. Neither English nor Scots. They straddle both worlds, and have the finesse of neither."

Juliana tossed her head. "I'll never kneel, and I'll never forgive any of you!"

"Suit yourself. Obviously pleasantries are wasted on you. Very well. We'll see what other kind of pleasures we can tempt you with."

This was going to be more fun, she thought.

"Bring wine!" Redbeard commanded his soldiers. "And prepare the wench for me."

"Prepare me yourself!"

Juliana watched as he undid his chainmail, and as it chinked to the floor, revealing broad shoulders beneath his leather tunic. Slowly he undid his tunic, exposing his naked chest, muscular, shining with strength, and promising stamina. For a moment, Juliana almost wished he was her captor. She fought for patience for she knew she was in for a good time.

Kicking off his boots, he loosened his breeches. Already they were tented at the front. Her fingers itched to touch it, her eyes longed to see it. And suddenly it was out. Erect and throbbing, with a purple head and a drip of moisture at the tip. It was certainly much bigger then she'd imagined. And his massive balls fascinated her. Large, perfectly oval, and covered in fine long hairs, she yearned to touch them, to feel their weight, to release them from the burden of their heavy load.

She'd never seen a man naked before, but this was beyond her wildest dreams. He turned around, to show small tight buttocks. Nice, but obviously the powerhouse was at the front. Facing her, he came towards her. She screwed her eyes tight trying to imagine Duncan naked in his place.

"Let me look at her!" growled Redbeard. A strong voice. A masterful voice.

The naked soldier took his knife from its scabbard and slit her blouse from throat to waist, revealing the top of her breasts, small, creamy, and high, held firm by their bodice.

Redbeard gave a curt nod to the other soldier who had already taken off his sword, and dropped it to the floor.

Dark-haired, with brown skin, and eyes as dark as an eastern sky, his manhood bulged through his outer garments, his breathing was already coming in harsh rasps. With a groan, he put his hand to his crotch and staggered towards her.

"Not yet, John," Redbeard cautioned. "You'll get your turn. You know what to do!"

With trembling fingers, John slid his knife between the laces of her bodice, pulled sharply once and the cut ribbons hung loose, freeing her peaked and hardened breasts. A warm thrill of fear coursed through her veins. These men certainly knew what they were about. Roughly John cupped her breast, his fingers circling her nipples, round and round, until they were erect and proud. Against her will, she pushed them forward.

John smiled. "She likes this!"

"They usually do."

They'd done this before!

Breathing heavily, he untied her wrists and ankles.

Now she had an inkling of what she was in for. This wasn't going to be like the frantic fumblings she'd witnessed in Scotland. This could be fun!

A picture of her parents flashed through her mind. Most certainly, they would expect her to try to escape. As would Duncan. She wavered, as another picture crossed her mind. Herself in ten years' time. Grown plump like her mother. Toil-weary and dressed in old clothes, collecting firewood at dawn and again at dusk. In the short term, what she had here was far more promising.

She couldn't keep her eyes from John's member, its head rearing almost to her waist. Her tongue crossed her upper lip in awe and anticipation as she reached for his manhood. She struggled to reach it, but was restrained by the imprisoning bonds. Seeing her distress, John untied the ropes at her wrists and she gratefully wrapped a hand around him.

Hard and sleek, it throbbed in her hand, the pulsing matching the pulling in her own belly. Inexperienced though she was, she knew she needed more.

"My, how the beauty of the face rivals the beauty of the body!" breathed Redbeard.

Juliana turned to look fully at him now, all thoughts of escape vanquished. Hair the colour of late autumn corn, beard as red and angry as a northern sunset, Redbeard was potent, menacing, as he advanced towards her. But it was his legs, strong and thick, widening slightly before they were hidden by his bear-skin tunic, that got most of her attention.

Pulling the pins from her hair, Redbeard drew his hands, rough but surprisingly tender, through it, allowing it to fall into a flaming cascade around her knees, enveloping them both. He picked it up, rubbing it softly against his face. "My men can have you first!"

Juliana licked her lips. She still had to see what Redbeard was like. His manner was certainly even more promising than the others. And they looked good!

The younger of the soldier opened a door off the bedchamber, leading to another room.

Juliana gaped in open-mouthed wonder.

"That's a special room where we keep the bath, my dear. We're going to teach you everything you'll ever need to know. It's a big bath, it'll take some time to fill it. In the meantime, to show you what a gentleman I am, I'm going to give you a drink."

Redbeard poured some wine into a goblet and held it to her lips. The wine was full-bodied, comforting.

"Juliana, we're going to see if we can make you into an English lady. If that's possible." He gestured the room. "All this is yours. And more." He held the goblet to her lips again. "If you don't, we'll return you to your village."

As the wine worked its way down her throat, it brought a feeling of warmth, relaxing her body, easing her mind.

"Redbeard?"

"Yes?"

"What about... I mean... I haven't seen... "

"Your inexperience is showing, dear. Along with your Scottish impatience." He picked her up and carried her over to an armchair by the fire.

Taking a comb off the table that held perfumed oils, Redbeard lightly but firmly pulled it through her hair removing the knots until it fell in a silken curtain around her body. The more he combed her hair, the more she relaxed. His touch was sensual, his smell spicy and exotic. His hands slowly circled her breasts, lingering, caressing, until she cried out for more. His hands shot around her waist and downwards, pulling off her skirt, leaving her naked.

Despite herself, she opened her legs.

But Redbeard wasn't going to spoil the fun.

He cupped her mound with his great hand.

"The hours of darkness are long, beauty. This is going to be your night of nights." His palm pressed firmly on her bush, his fingers parting her nether lips, until her slim hips twitched beneath him and she gasped, as moisture touched the tops of her thighs.

He rose from between her legs and walked over to the silver tray of fruit. As he went, she watched the enormous bulge beneath his belt, building his tunic into a tent.

Kneeling before her, he fed the grape from his mouth to hers, his hands caressing her hair and her rosy peaks.

"You always have a choice, beauty. I'm not a man to rape a woman."

A tear of frustration slipped from Juliana's eye and ran down her cheek. Redbeard caught it on his finger and he licked it off.

"But I am a man who keeps his word. And I promise you, this night you'll not be disappointed! But you do have a choice! It's up to you!"

He knelt between her legs again, stroking the underside of her thighs. As he did so, his bearskin rode up slightly, and something as hot as a newly baked loaf and as hard as a mace rested on top of her thighs.

Juliana slid down in the armchair to better feel him with her thighs.

"Soon, beauty, soon."

Juliana's lip trembled as she felt more moisture

trickle from her thighs on to the chair below.

"Sire, the bath's ready."

"God's blood," Redbeard hissed as he rose and moved away from her.

"Go with Jake, beauty."

Juliana looked up to see Jake, the blond soldier standing naked before her. Clothed, he'd been handsome. Naked, he was Adonis.

Redbeard helped her to her shaky legs. As she stood unclothed before him, she watched in amazement as Jake sucked in a deep breath, his manhood swelling from flaccid to erect, from calm to angry.

"With Jake?"

"Jake first."

Juliana didn't know where to turn, so great was her joy. What she needed was relief.

Quickly pursued by Jake, she ran to the bed and lay spread-eagled on her back. Jake mounted her immediately, only for Redbeard to pull him away.

"Bathe her first, you idiot!"

Shamefacedly, Jake took her hand and led her to the privy room while his other hand cradled his member.

The bath water was warm, full of bubbles, smelt faintly of roses, as he lowered her into it. Redbeard watched as Jake and John bathed her. At the same time, Jake washed her hair, massaging her scalp until she felt so relaxed she could almost sleep. Then Jake washed her body, his firm hands cleaning her, his fingers exploring every bodily orifice until her body and soul cried out for release.

Redbeard held the goblet to her lips once more. "Drink while we prepare you for the pleasures of the English!"

Juliana reclined in the tub, happy to allow these men to take control.

Carefully and tenderly Redbeard soaped her arms. "There's nothing to be afraid of. Indeed, soon you'll beg me not to stop." He feathered his fingers over her breasts, each one in turn, circling with his strong fingers until her nipples were hard and taut.

Now it was John's turn. He stroked her hair, her arms, her belly, his hand exploring lower to where the dark curls lay in a wet triangle. He parted her thighs, his fingers skimming her secret places, probing with his fingers, seeking, pleasuring. Juliana gasped with joy.

Redbeard brushed her wet hair back with his strong hands. "Beauty, you're as lovely as the sunrise!"

Juliana glanced at Jake, his face a contorted picture of agony.

"Can I have her now, master?" he gasped.

"Not yet,' breathed Redbeard. 'It's John's turn next."

John came to lift her out of the bath. Although less handsome than Jake, he was a far bigger man. He picked her up her body, wet and slippery, and carrying her to the bed, lay her face down upon the silken sheets and straddled her.

Juliana groaned at the pleasure of a man's weight on top of her, and tried to turn over to receive him.

But John's hands, capable and sensitive, massaged perfumed oil into her shoulders, relaxing some muscles, awakening others. His clever fingers feathered down her spine, her buttocks, her thighs, as wave after wave of pleasure coursed through her body. Then he turned her over on to her back.

Through eyes tinted with desire, she viewed her

three men.

Jake, young and beautiful, still in delicious pain, his hands clasping and unclasping at his swollen member.

Then John, older, bigger, heavier. His hands played so many clever, magical tricks with her body she never wanted him to stop.

And Redbeard. Unviewed, untried, but promising myriad delights.

Desperate now, she put her hand between her legs, parted her rose lips, and ran a finger into her cleft, seeking satisfaction. With lightning speed, Redbeard moved and withdrew her finger.

"No, dearest, the time has not yet come. You must have patience."

Smiling he undid the belt around his bearskin, unfastened it at the shoulder. It fell to the ground. His body was magnificent. Strong, controlled, he was by far the biggest of them all.

John and Jake, she wanted. They could give her instant relief.

"I promised you a choice. Which one of us do you want?"

Juliana groaned her frustration. She also wanted Redbeard but wasn't sure she could handle so virile a man.

"Can... can I have you all?"

Redbeard smiled. "No."

A sob of frustration escaped her lips. "I ... I can't... "

"You can, and you will."

"I can't choose."

"You can't have us all at once. It's obvious. However, you can and you will, have us all. Each in turn."

Juliana sighed contentedly.

John and Jake took a slim ankle each, and using silken scarves, tethered each ankle to a bedpost. Redbeard knelt on the great bed between her spread legs, his middle leg so thick she wondered if she'd be able to take it all. He bound each of her wrists to the top of the bedposts. His manhood nuzzled her womanly lips. Slowly, tantalisingly, he entered her, pushing deeper, deeper. He stopped.

"A virgin, eh? Don't worry, beauty. First you'll feel pain, then unsurpassed joy."

With a jolt, he thrust forward. Heat and pain flowed through her small body and Juliana thought she would burst. Then joy and sweetness, as pleasure surged through her young body.

As she was riding a wave of sensation, cresting to ecstasy, Redbeard pulled away, leaving her muscles clamping around the empty air. Frantic, Juliana tried to pull him back.

"Wait, darling, these men have been patient."

Limping off the bed, Redbeard made way for Jake, the youngest of the trio.

"God, but you're lovely," he muttered as, without preamble, he thrust into her, his member stretching and swelling inside her as he thrust and sweated, called her name, and fell gasping on top of her.

Redbeard and John lifted him off.

Now it was John's turn.

Carefully, he kissed her hairline, her ears, her nose, massaged her arms and her legs, laved her rosebud breasts and entered her suddenly, his body spasming as again and again he bucked.

Juliana knew that this giving of pleasure must be her true calling in life. She had finally come home!

But there was still something. Something she

needed for herself, but she was too inexperienced to know what it was.

"Tired yet?" asked Redbeard.

"No, my lord," she said. "As you said, the night is long. Let's use it to best advantage."

With infinite care, Redbeard undid all the bonds that tied her to the bed.

"You've been a good girl to my men," he whispered. "Now it's my turn to show our thanks."

From the depths of Juliana's soul rose a mixture of anticipation and excitement she would never have dreamed possible.

Disbelief and joy thrilled through Juliana. Could there possibly be more?

Using a damp cloth he wiped her brow, kissing her hairline, eyelids, eyelashes, caressing her ears, teasing the insides of them with his fingers, then his lips teased hers. Juliana parted her lips and he kissed her tenderly, then deeply. With their tongues entwined, she raised her knees to wrap them around his great body. Firm hands caressed her thighs, the flare of her hips. Softly, his lips caressed her breasts, bringing them to throbbing peaks.

His mouth moved downwards, flooding the slight indentation of her navel, to her damp curls and beyond, and parting her folds, his tongue pushed and teased until she cried out with joy. And just as she thought there could be further happiness in life, Redbeard entered her. Bigger by far than his soldiers, her muscles clamped down on him as he rode her rhythmically, forcefully, showing her who was truly in charge. Again and again, he drove into her. Again and again, she cried out her pleasure to the night.

Finally, with her legs shaking, when she thought she could do no more, Redbeard rode her, taking her on wave after wave of pleasure until she could die of ecstasy, and they lay together on the great bed, gasping and laughing, their souls filled with satisfaction and contentment.

"I said I'd give you a choice," murmured Redbeard. "Instead, I'll give you several."

But Juliana had a few tricks of her own.

"No, my lord, it is I who will give you some choices."

Sitting at the foot of the bed, she secured his legs, then his arms, to the bedposts.

Lowering her head to his manhood, she put her lips over his throbbing, erect member, thrilled at her ability to make him stiffen, then harden once more. Slowly she ran her tongue around his tip, down his shaft, up again.

When her newly-experienced psyche judged the time right, she caressed his member with her arm-pits, breasts, ears, and feeling his climax approaching again, she straddled him, lowering herself, massaging him with her womanly muscles.

And pulled away.

"About my having the makings of an English Lady... "

"Please... " he gasped.

"Do you want me?"

"Yes."

"As a lady?"

"For God's sake... "

She lowered herself on to him again, holding his tip firm, sliding down slowly,

"Are you sending me back to my village?"

As she sank herself further on to his shaft, Redbeard pulled her down, reared and sweated beneath her, taking her with him on a tidal wave of pleasure.

In that delirious moment, Juliana knew this was where she belonged.

Michael J Richards

Mike won first prize in his university's short story competition; he edited his tutor's book on Joseph Conrad. He has written and directed a play about Anthony and Cleopatra, two satirical revues and two pantomimes (in which he played the dame).

He has written six novels and thrown them away – they were rubbish – and two unbroadcast radio plays, one about the 1980s Miners' Strike and the other about Henry Bellingham, the assassin of the Prime Minster, Spencer Percival.

In 2005, he contributed the chapter on mechanical engineering in *Information Sources in Engineering*, pub K G Saur Verlag.

In 2014, he published a comic horror novel, *Afterwards Our Buildings Shape Us*. He has acted in two short films, *Nyctophobia* (2014) and *Closed Circuit* (2015) and has recently completed his first film as Writer/Director, *The Isolated Essence of a Subject*.

He is planning to publish an anthology of his own short stories in 2016.

Mike is Chair of Northampton Literature Group and a member of three writers' groups, two of which (Northants Writers' Ink, and Northampton Literature Group's Writers' Circle), he is Chair/leader.

Where do we go from here?

by Michael J Richards

"Hungry?" she says.

"Nah," he drawls. "Not really." He lets out a lazy, lingering yawn.

"I've picked this fruit from the garden," she says. "I want you to taste it, to see what it's like. I think it's the best we've ever had."

"Later… later," he says. "Come here. It's too hot to do anything like hard work. In this heat, eating is hard work."

She lays down the fruit and comes over to him. They sprawl on the succulent grass.

"Isn't this great!" he says. "Nothing to do but enjoy the afternoon. Do you know, I think afternoon is my favourite time of day. We've done our work and now the rest of the day is ours. Laying here in the sun, seeing the plants grow, watching the animals, listening to the birds. Look at the sun! Not a cloud in the sky. Can you see any clouds?"

"No, darling," she murmurs, staring at his bronzing body. "I can't see any."

"D'y'know, I can't believe how lucky we are. Just you and me, pussy cat. No-one here to bother us. Just you and me in our own world. Paradise on earth."

She smooths her hand over his chest. "You are so beautiful," she says. "I adore your chest. Where did you get a chest like that? You've really caught the sun." Her hands move over him, gently feeling her way over his torso. "I've never seen a chest like this anywhere."

"Well, that's true," he laughs with delight. "And what's more, you'll never see another like it anywhere else!"

She grabs his thighs. "And legs, what legs. So firm, so muscular, so strong. Like a big brown bear."

He sits up, pulling his legs apart to keep balance and remain upright, inspecting her hands as they hold on to his thighs. "Well, they're all right. I've never really noticed my legs. To me, they're just hairy limbs that let me walk and run and climb trees and do the stuff legs are supposed to do."

"Oh no," she says. "They're more than that. They're part of what makes you so handsome. I love your legs. Your beautiful, beautiful… legs. Who'd've thought legs could be so bewitchingly beautiful. They can take us anywhere we want to go." She runs her hands down towards his feet, bends over and lightly kisses each knee. She peers up at him, giggling.

He falls back, also laughing, his legs splaying out almost at right angles to each other. As a sigh comes from the depths of his spirit, he closes his eyes and wraps an arm around her as she, too, closes her eyes.

They remain still, in union, as they bathe in the bright yellow sun, on the featherlight grass, under the drowsingly cobalt sky, within the lusciously warm breeze.

After a few minutes of lazy idling, she sits upright, looking about her, as if she has heard something.

From the near distance, a green and purple bird flaps and squawks its way towards them, hovers and then glides and lands a few feet away. It stands, staring at them, head cocked to one side.

"Oh!" she squeals, clapping her hands. "It's a – it's – what do you call it?"

He rouses himself up and rests back on his elbows. "Oh, that. I call it a parakeet."

"What a pretty name for a pretty creature." She mouths the word slowly to herself, as if hearing it for the first time. "Come here, pretty parakeet."

The parakeet creeps forwards and, as she leans over to stroke it, it opens its wings and flies upwards, away into the sky.

"It goes so high," she murmurs. "How does it get so high? Shall we ever get so high?"

"Why do you want to – I mean, we're happy here, aren't we? Come here, my little guinea pig."

But she is not satisfied. "It must be so wonderful to be able to get so high – to go so far away. All we ever do is stay here."

"Here is fine. Here is good. Here is where we are. Come here. Give me your arms."

She shakes her head with a violence she never knew she had – and which, for the first time in his life, shocks him. "Ha! Here is where we always are," she says, pouting. "Never there. Why can't we be there? Just once. Just for once, I want to be there. To see what it's like. That's all I ask. I mean, tell me, is that too much to ask?"

"Oh, my turtle dove, come here," he urges. "We're happy here, aren't we? You've always said you like it here. Let's be happy with where we are."

He lies back, his sun-burnished body inviting her enrapture, his black hair falling back to open his face out into the blazing heat. She turns to take in his hair-covered body.

But her meditation is interrupted by more flapping and squawking in the sky. She looks up to see, now, two parakeets flying through the air, side by side, opal green wings outstretched, flying so close to each other they are as one with one mind. Their pale green heads turn to see each other and, as they do so, they let out a unison echoing cry of such intimacy that it possesses the blueness of the air around, above and below them.

"Ooh!" she cries out. "Do you see that?"

But he sees nothing. His eyes are closed. "What?"

"See the – what are they?"

"Para – "

" – keet – I remember now. Para – "

" – keet," he finishes, still not opening his eyes.

"Parakeet, parakeet, parakeet, parakeet… What a pretty name for a pretty bird," she burbles, bouncing up and down with the joy of a new discovery. "Parakeet, parakeet, I love parakeet."

She rests back as she watches the two birds playing in the breeze, snuggling up to each other, then drawing away only to enjoy coming together again. Then, suddenly, one of them circles the other several times before disappearing into the distance, the other following until they are out of sight, as if they have never existed.

"Oh," she says, shedding a tiny tear. "They've gone… oh," – and she frumps back, the excitement over. She picks at the grass. "Don't you wish we were like that?"

"Like what?"

"The birds. Then we could fly away, like them, leave here and go and find new places… and do new things."

His eyes are still closed. "We're all right here."

"Even so," she says. "I mean, can't we just once be somewhere else, go somewhere else, like those –

those – "

"Parakeets."

She nods hurriedly before she forgets. "Yes, of course. Silly me. Parakeets."

"We're all right here."

She looks him over. "I'm beautiful, aren't I? You do think I'm beautiful, don't you?"

He opens his eyes and stretches out his hand to stroke her flowing yellow hair. "Yes, my little piglet, you are very beautiful."

"And," she adds, "you do love me, don't you? Say you love me."

"You know I do."

She turns away and is startled to see the fruit, as if it has miraculously appeared from nowhere. She picks it up.

"I picked this fruit from the garden. I want you to taste it, to see what it's like. It's the best we've ever had."

He sits up and adjusts his body to sit cross-legged. "All right, then, give it here, let's have a look."

She holds out the fruit. "It's the best we've ever had."

He reaches out and takes it. He brings it slowly towards his face. "I don't remember seeing this before." He sinks his teeth into it, takes a mouthful, chews it around. "Mmm, not bad." He chews. He swallows.

His brain empties. His throat vibrates. His chest shakes. His groin quivers. His legs and feet tremble. He tries to keep balance. But his soul goes down, down his throat, through his body, down and through and down… and down. Rivulets of sweat cascade over him. And then, just as instantly, he shivers, and comes to. He looks down and lets out a screeching groan. He stands up, frightened, not knowing where to put his hands – but now and forever and always knowing exactly where to put his hands.

"Aah!" he screams. He looks about him, like a doomed victim, a hunted rabbit fearful for its life. "Oh, my fragrant tempting angel, what have you done?" He draws himself up, his eyes flitting everywhere, searching for hungry wolves. "We have to go."

"Go? I don't want to go. I like it here."

"Oh no, no, no, no, no!" he shouts. "You wanted to go. Well, you get your wish. We've got to go or we'll get caught – "

"Caught? What – "

"Can't you see? Look at us. I mean, look at us! Get up. Get up!" He pulls her up. "Leave the fruit. Put it down. Do as I tell you, can't you. Don't touch it. We have to go."

As she looks down to see the fruit roll away, her right arm covers her breasts, her left moves to hide her groin. She stares up at him. They stand, unable to move. They turn away, not knowing which way to go, not knowing what to do, realising they no longer have anything to say to each other. She bows her head as tears flowed silently, uncontrollably.

"Oh, Adam," she whispers. "Where do we go from here?"

He shakes his head, lost, bewildered, broken. "God only knows."

Lost in a Fog

by Michael J Richards

"Mummy," says Patrick, "why is Patrick in the bathroom?"

Mummy answers from the kitchen. "Clean your teeth, darling."

"Clean your teeth," Patrick says.

He takes the top off the tube and squeezes its middle. He picks up his teddy bear yellow toothbrush and watches the toothpaste fall on to the white bristles.

He hears Mummy come into the bathroom.

"Look, Mummy. Patrick is cleaning his teeth," he says.

Mummy looks. She wipes his mouth with a towel. "Get your coat."

"Patrick isn't cold," he says.

"We're going to see the doctor. It's cold and foggy and it's a long walk."

"Can Patrick wear his hoodie, Mummy? Patrick wants to wear his hoodie. Patrick likes his hoodie."

"Yes, all right," she sighs. "If you want to."

"Patrick's a good boy, isn't he?"

"Yes, darling. You're a good boy," Mummy says.

* * * * *

Mummy looks in her bag to make sure she has

everything. She takes Patrick out of the flat and shuts the door.

She sighs. Her mouth lets out a little cloud. She looks at her watch. "We're in good time," she says. "It's still only ten minutes past nine." She yawns.

The thick fog makes it hard for Patrick to see where he is going. He holds out his hand because Mummy has told him to hold her hand when they are out.

Mummy looks at him. "Your glasses are crooked," she says. "Come here." Every day, every hour, she has to put them right so he can see. "There, that's better."

"That's better," he says.

"Come on," she says. "Give me your hand. Let's go."

"Let's go," he says.

* * * * *

When they are walking along, Patrick says, "What's that?" He has stopped and is staring down.

A big lady carrying a big blue bag bumps into him from behind.

"Look where you're going, can't you?" she says.

He does not look up. "Get off!" he shouts, shaking and crying. "Get off me or I'll hit you. Patrick is looking at this."

The big lady carrying the big blue bag looks Patrick up and down and backs away.

"I'm so sorry," Mummy says. "He won't hurt you."

"Patrick won't hurt you," he says.

The big lady with the big blue bag hurries by, getting smaller as she waddles into the thick fog.

186

"Patrick," Mummy says, now at a stop because he is still staring down but not crying. "You mustn't stop like that. You mustn't talk to people like that. It's very naughty."

"Look at that," he says.

Mummy looks at the spot that he is staring at so hard. "What can you see, darling?" she says.

A big rolling monster shakes by, sending out black smoke from its bottom. Patrick looks up, shocked. He turns and watches as it gets smaller and smaller in the shivering fog. "What's that?" he shouts. "What's that?"

"A lorry, dear, that's all, a lorry," she says, pulling at her gloves. "Let's get on."

Patrick does not move. He screams at the fog, "Mummy, help Patrick. The face is going to eat me all up!"

"We haven't time for that now," Mummy says. "We'll look at it when we come back."

As she pulls him away, he falls into a trot to keep up. "Where are we going?" he says.

She does not look at him. "I told you," she shouts through the fog as she pulls him along. "The nice doctor's going to make sure you're well."

"Nice doctor."

"Yes, darling," she says, as he holds her hand tightly. "Nice doctor."

* * * * *

The nice doctor says something to Mummy that makes her smile. Then he says something to Patrick. Mummy sits down so Patrick sits down. The doctor is being nice to Mummy, which Patrick does not like, so he makes a face at him. But the doctor does not see, because he is still talking to Mummy.

The horrid doctor says some more things and then Mummy says some more things. They use long words. Patrick does not like people who use long words. Except Mummy, of course. He likes everything about Mummy.

"Thank you, doctor," Mummy says.

"All right," he says, looking at Patrick. "Take off your coat."

Patrick stands up. "It's not a coat, it's a hoodie, isn't it, Mummy?"

The bossy doctor is looking at Mummy. Patrick looks at Mummy. She is yawning again. She stands up so Patrick stands up. The doctor says something and then Mummy says something but he cannot hear through his hoodie.

"Come on, Patrick," Mummy says, "let's get your hoodie and your tee-shirt off. Arms up." He holds up his arms. She looks down. She turns away from him and says to the doctor, "Oh, I'm so sorry."

The doctor looks up from his computer and looks at Patrick. "Don't worry," he says.

"I've got some dry clothes and a towel here," Mummy says. "I always carry them. It's always like this. I'm sorry. Come on, Patrick, let's get you out of those things."

Patrick says, "Patrick is wet. Patrick is sorry."

The doctor goes red and he looks at the words on his computer. Mummy takes off all of Patrick's clothes and makes him dry again.

Then the doctor turns to look at them. "Okay, young man," he says, standing up and breathing on a silver ring on the end of two long black snakes around his neck, "Let's see how you've been getting on."

* * * * *

Later, Mummy helps Patrick to get dressed. The kind doctor who has warm hands makes words come up on his computer. He says something but does not look at Mummy, which Patrick thinks is rude. Mummy always says to look at who you are talking to.

"I can't," she says, doing up Patrick's trousers. "He's lost without me."

The doctor says she must go to the seaside without Patrick. Patrick must make his own friends. It is wrong for Mummy to be Patrick's only friend.

"If you say so, doctor," says Mummy as she carries on dressing Patrick.

The nosy doctor asks Mummy when she last went to the seaside.

Patrick does not like the doctor talking to Mummy and not to Patrick so he says, "It's Patrick's birthday tomorrow, isn't it, Mummy?"

The doctor says to Patrick, "And how old you will be?"

"I don't know."

Staring at the floor, Mummy says, "Of course you do, darling. You'll be twenty-four, won't you?"

As Mummy stands up, she pulls his tee-shirt down his front to make him look nice. She holds on to his broad shoulders so she does not fall.

Patrick says, "Mummy, why are you crying?"

Learnin' the family business

by Michael J Richards

"Lose control – "

"Sure, Joey."

"–and you're in deep trouble," I say. "*Buongiorno*, Signora Mamazza." I raise my homberg.

She smiles. "*Buongiorno*, Joey."

"Can Stefano assist you with your shoppin'?"

"No, it's fine, Joey, *grazie*."

"Stefano," I say, "are you blind or sumpthin? I'm sorry, Signora Mamazza, Stefano aint learnt yet to respect our senior citizens. You buffoon," I shout, slappin' him on his head, "assist Mrs Mamazza's with her shoppin'."

"Sure, Joey."

As my kid brother takes the shoppin' and escorts Mrs Mamazza across the street and up the steps, I lean against the door of Mr Balduccio's bakery and light up a Chesterfield. Once the old lady is indoors, Stefano runs back.

"You gotta show respect," I tell him. "It's important you keep the goodwill of the neighbour-hood. They gotta know they can come to you. That way, you own the streets you walk. Y'unnerstand?"

"Yeah, Joey," he says. "Thanks, Joey."

I stub out my butt-end with my shoe. "Now I'm gonna show you how to collect."

A bell clangs as we go into Mr Balducci's shop

and we're surrounded by bread like you never seen nowhere on God's earth. Ciabatta, buccellato, focaccia, muffuletta, pane di Altamura, sgabeo, michetta – and more. The aromas send me crazy. Sometimes, I think Mr Balducci is my favourite client.

"Joey, Joey, Joey!" he calls, as he comes from the back. He's a short, round man with a walrus moustache and bushes of black hair on each side of his bald head. His white apron, hands and arms are covered in flour. Dobs of flour decorate his face like we interrupt make-up for a clown act.

"Mr Balducci, this is my brother, Stefano."

"Che bel giovane!"

"Mr Balducci," I say, "we speak English in our new country."

"Naturalmente, come stupido da parte mia." He shakes Stefano's hand. "He is like you, Joey... but maybe younger."

"Seven years," I say. "And now he's sixteen, he's learnin' the family business."

"Oh," Mr Balducci says, his mouth quiverin'. *"Questo è molto buono."*

"Yeah," my brother pipes up.

"So what happens now, Stefano, is Mr Balducci hands over his *pizzo*." I look at the baker. "Dya hear me? I said, 'Mr Balducci hands over his *pizzo*.'"

"Twenty bucks," Stefano says.

"Good boy," I say. "Learnin' fast."

Mr Balducci brings out a tin box and counts out twenty bones. He pushes the cash towards me. I stretch out and hold down the greens and his hand so he can't move.

"But, Stefano," I say, grippin' the baker's hand, "sometimes they forget or they aint ready for us. Mr

Balducci aint ready for us. That shows disrespect. It tells me Mr Balducci don't wanna be protected against citizens who come in to injure him. And that," I continue, bendin' back his middle finger, "is bad news for a man who lives by his hands."

"Are you gonna break his fingers?"

As I watch Mr Balducci's face, I bend the finger back a bit more. He's sweatin' like a pig that knows it ends up on my dinner plate. "Wassup, Mr Balducci? You nervous or sumpthin?"

"*Per favore*, Joey," he whines. "I have the *pizzo*. How can I be ready when I don't know when you come? You break my fingers, I make no more bread, you get no more *pizzo*."

I hold him tight for a few seconds, laugh, lower his finger but don't let go. "You see, Stefano, many times you don't do nuttin'. It's enough the client knows you would."

"Yeah," says Stefano.

"Your turn."

He steps forward. As I let go, he grabs the old man's hand. "Like this?" And with his other hand, he grips Mr Balducci's index finger and bends it back.

"Yeah, that's it. You got it… Some more. You can always go some more."

Stefano stretches the finger back some more. "Yeah," he says, lowerin' his face to look closely. "I see what you mean." He looks up at Mr Balducci and smiles. "How's that for you?"

"*Sei un bravo studente*," he whimpers, his shirt soakin' under his arms and on his belly.

"*Basta*, Stefano," I say. "We got other clients to see."

* * * * *

192

Mr D'Ambrosio calls a meet of his closest associates. That's Lefty, Kid Face, Too Quick, Freckles and Wassup. And me, o' course. Stefano asks if he can come but I tell him he can when he's bin made.

"The Blumberg Boys are gettin' too big," Mr D'Ambrosio says, "and if we don't move in, they give us trouble. Morey Blumberg holds a pow-wow with four of his closest tomorrow night." He rubs his nose. "And you boys are gonna wipe 'em out."

"Why not tonight, Mr D'Ambrosio?" Lefty says.

"Tomorrow's the funeral of the Valentino kid," he says. "The cops'll be too busy worryin' about mopin' girls to pay attention to what's goin' on the other side o' town. The rest o' you, meet here at seven, tooled up. You do everythin' Lefty tells ya. Meantime, go spend time with your families. Take 'em to Coney Island or sumpthin. And talk to nobody. Too Quick, Freckles, Kid Face, Wassup – get out. I wanna speak to Lefty and Pretty Boy."

They leave the room.

"Hey, close the door, can't ya."

"Sorry, Mr D'Ambrosio," Kid Face says, closin' the door.

Mr D'Ambrosio leans forward. "Now listen to me good. One o' them four is on Morey's payroll. But I don't know who. The six of you take out the Blumbergs. After they're down, you nail the traitor and he don't ride back with ya. And make sure the others see what's goin' on."

I fall back in my seat.

"You gotta problem, Pretty Boy?"

"What if we can't nail him?"

Mr D'Ambrosio shakes his head. "If you can't do that simple thing, then you don't come back neither." He looks me straight in the eye. "Y'unnerstan'?"

"Yes, Mr D'Ambrosio."

"We don't carry no spare baggage, do we, Lefty?"

"No, Mr D'Ambrosio, we don't," Lefty says. "How dya get the lowdown on all o' this?"

"Herbie Blumberg's on my payroll."

* * * * *

"So you stay with Ma tonight," I tell Stefano. "You don't talk enough to Ma. She worries."

"Where you goin'?"

"Gotta do sumpthin for Mr D'Ambrosio."

"If I come, I learn some more."

"If you don't come, you stay alive. Help Ma bake a cake."

"Aw, Joey."

"Aw, nuttin'."

Soon, the boys and me are ridin' along in our Packard Phaeton. Lefty's at the wheel 'cos he's the only one who knows the location and he aint tellin'. Kid Face asks where we're goin' but Lefty tells him to keep his mouth shut, he'll find out soon enough.

After a while, Lefty slows down, turns off the headlights and coasts to the opposite side of the road to a Jewish restaurant, where he parks. It's a dark joint next to a row of shops and then there's a scrub of land with tumbleweed and a mean crouchin' dog snarlin' at insects. Night is almost here.

"You sure this is the joint?" Too Quick says.

"Course it's the joint," Lefty snaps. "You think I'm dumb?"

"No, no," Too Quick says too quick. "Only there's no-one there."

"That space there is where we do the job," Lefty says. "Freckles, Kid Face, go bring 'em out."

They cross the street with their Thompson M1921s, knock on the door. They wait. The door opens. Freckles and Kid Face go in. There's some bawlin' and shoutin' but soon eight men come out, hands in the air, Freckles and Kid Face behind 'em, weapons aimed at their backs. The rest of us cross the street and, usin' our Thompsons, get 'em on to the scrub. The mangy mutt jumps forward, barkin', but Freckles gives it a hefty kick and sends it flyin'.

We line 'em up, their noses touchin' the restaurant wall.

Freckles, Kid Face, Too Quick and Wassup empty their drums at 'em, with Lefty and me holdin' back. Nobody cares about the racket. Nobody's gonna come out and see what's goin' on.

It's all over in five minutes.

The boys stand over their handiwork, grinnin' like cats what've found a stash o' cream at the bottom of an empty coffin. They spend a few seconds laughin' and sploshin' about in the blood and guts and brains.

Lefty and me let 'em have their minute o' fun. After all, it's the last minute they're gonna get.

"Boys," Lefty says, "we got homes to go to."

Lefty and me raise our Thompsons.

Freckles, Kid Face, Too Quick and Wassup look up.

"Wassup?" Wassup says.

"Okay, who's the rat?" Lefty says.

The four of 'em stare at us, then each other.

"What's goin' on?" Kid Face says. "Wha' choo talkin' about?"

"C'm' on, boys, don't mess me about. One o' you's on the Blumberg payroll. Who is it?"

Nobody speaks.

We're standin' there like kids playin' at cowboys

195

in a schoolyard, nobody movin', nobody squawkin'.

"I'll count to three and if the rat don't speak up, Pretty Boy and me'll decide. And the three who aint the rat don't want that, do they? Whoever the rat is, the others know. So, last chance, boys, who is it?"

"It aint me, Lefty," Too Quick splutters. "I'm good."

"One."

"You gotta believe me," he says. "Mr D'Ambrosio's my uncle, for chrissake, he's family –"

"Two."

Kid Face's cryin' and fallin' to his knees. "On my ma's grave – "

"Three."

"Okay, Pretty Boy," Lefty says –

"Oh God – "

" – let's finish this – "

While Lefty takes out Freckles and Wassup, I get Too Quick and Kid Face. Down they go, like swatted bluebottles. Now it's their blood and guts and brains spreadin' everywhere.

"Too bad," Lefty says. "I really liked Kid Face."

"Me, too."

"Such a great kisser, too," he says. "Finished?"

"Let's get outa here."

We head towards the Packard.

"You hear sumpthin?" Lefty says.

We stop and listen. It's like a girl bawlin'.

"Who's there?" Lefty calls out, pullin' out his Colt pistol.

The bawlin' carries on. "Joey – "

We go around on to the sidewalk. Stefano's slumped on the ground, leanin' up against the Packard. The streetlamp catches him.

He's snivellin' and sniffin', wipin' his face with

his sleeve. He looks up at me. "Joey – " he cries. "I'm sorry, I just wanted to – "

"How'd you get here?" I say. I grab Lefty's arm. "Put that away."

Lefty lowers his aim. "Yeah, how'd you get here?"

"I hid in the trunk," Stefano says. "I wanted to be – I thought if I came – then – I could... You two are my heroes. I'd do anythin' to be like you."

Lefty looks at me and back at Stefano. "Aint gonna happen, kid. Y'see, we don't allow no witnesses. You know that, Pretty Boy. You shoulda told him."

"He's my brother," I whisper. "For chrissake, Lefty."

"I don't care if he's your ma on crutches and your old granny in a wheelchair," he says, raisin' the Colt. "No witnesses is no witnesses." He takes aim.

"No!" Stefano screams, scrabblin' to get away.

I drop my Thompson and lunge at Lefty. As he falls on his side, the pistol fires. A coupla seconds later, glass shatters somewhere. Lefty's on the ground, he's dropped his Thompson and he's dropped his Colt, it goes skatin' across the sidewalk into the streetlamp's yellow light.

I throw myself at the pistol and get it before Lefty can move. I pick up my homberg. I aint in no hurry standin' up. I put the homberg on, wipe my mouth, move out the light. "Stefano, get in the car."

"Joey – "

"I said, get in the car."

He crawls into the car. "Joey – "

Lefty don't move. "Pretty Boy – "

"Yeah, I know."

As I get him between the eyes, I jump away so his blood don't get on me.

I pick up the Thompsons, climb into the Packard, start it up and Stefano and me get outa there.

Reading the Map Upside-down

by Michael J Richards

As I switch on the bedside lamp, Pete says, "That's the last time I share a room with you. I didn't get a minute's shut-eye." He sits up. "Why didn't tell me you snore?"

"You didn't ask."

He pushes his right hand through his black curly hair, his left pulls at his beard. "Not a good way to start the day."

I'm standing between our single beds. "C'm' on, get up."

He looks me up and down. "For chrissake, it's the middle of October. Aren't you cold, you hairless wimp?"

"No, but I soon will be, and so will you, if we don't get a move on."

He pulls himself up. "Yeah... You're right." He falls back, yawning. "We're good for another half-hour or so."

I make for the bathroom. "C'm' on, Muscles."

"For Christ's sake," he says, looking at his watch.

"You said five o'clock. I didn't."

I'm downstairs getting breakfast while Pete sorts himself out. In the time it takes me to do everything, he's still cleaning his teeth and not yet in the shower. At long last, he comes into the kitchen, a towel wrapped around him, dripping wet - he hasn't even dried himself.

He sits at the table. "Orange juice. Where's the orange juice?" he says. "How can you forget the orange juice?"

"It's coming, it's coming." I place a glass of orange juice on to the table.

"Not like that," he blubs. As he stands up, his towel loosens. He takes a deep inward breath and lets out an enormous sigh. He re-arranges the table so the orange juice stands in the centre, the rest of the food in a perfect circle around it. He sits down.

I pour myself some orange juice and plonk it on to the table.

He stands up again, verging on fury. He picks up the toast and the muesli, goes over to the pedal bin and throws the lot away. He pours both orange juices down the sink.

"Now, you addle-brained piece of horseshit," he says, "get it right." He sits down, sweating and near to tears. He tries to wipe his face with his towel but it tangles in the chair, his legs, his arms and, finally, around his head. "Oh, for – " – wrestles with it, pulls it off and throws it across the room.

I keep quiet. It's what I expected. I make breakfast again, placing each item on the kitchen table as I go along. He inspects the finished result, nods, looks up and smiles, his white teeth shining through his black moustache and beard, his chest hair glistening from the remains of his shower.

"That's a real treat, Mark. Thanks."

We eat in silence – apart from his overcompensating crunching of toast and slurping of orange juice. I make the tea.

He sits back, picking at his teeth. "Isn't life wonderful?" he says. "Well," he says at last, getting up, the towel long forgotten. "I'll get some kit on."

When he comes back, I've checked and packed up my* gear, ready to go into the early morning darkness. I'm washing up the breakfast things and putting them on the side so I don't have to come back to them. For all of Pete's anxieties about things having to be in their place, he doesn't give a thought about tidying up. I haven't touched the towel.

"Are we ready?" I say, putting the last teaspoon on the drying-rack.

"Just gotta check my gear."

Sighing, I put down the tea-towel. "Pete, you checked it last night, you checked it just now, didn't you? You did, didn't you? Don't you think – "

"Marky baby," he says as he lays his stuff out on the table, "take a tip from an old pro. You can't check your gear too many times."

I stand next to him and pat him on the back. "You're obsessing over nothing."

I know he's ignoring me. He pulls a piece of paper and pen from his pocket. He points to each item with the pen and ticks it off. "First aid kit, one. Water-bottles, water, filled with, three. Sandwiches, jam, raspberry, four. Map, one. Compass, one. Flares, three. Mobile, one. Camera, one. Batteries, camera, six. Binoculars, one."

As he packs up his stuff, he smiles. "Who's driving?"

"Me yesterday. You today."

He drives like a deranged drunk. But he always does. It's still pitch dark, he's going too fast and these Welsh country lanes are so narrow there's no room for anyone to get by.

"You are allowed to drive slowly," I tell him.

Without slowing down, he twists the car into a

small clearing at the side of the road and stops with an alarming shudder. He grinds the car into reverse, veers to the left, pulls against a grass verge and switches off the ignition.

"If you park over there," I say, pointing to a small lay-by next to a wall, "you'll be off the road. Much safer."

Without a word, he starts up the engine and puts the car facing a wall. Leaving the lights on, he gets out. "The sun's coming up," he says. "By the time we're geared up, the light will be good. C'm' on. Look lively."

He's right. It takes us a good twenty minutes to sort ourselves out and get our bearings. He puts his map, torch and compass in easily accessible backpack pockets, switches off the lights and locks the car.

"Ready?" he says.

I nod. I'm ready. I ought to be. We've been planning this for weeks. Well, Pete has. When you get climbs like this, it's better to be with someone who's experienced and willing to guide and help you improve. Everyone goes wrong at some time or other – or, worse, gets lost or falls. Everyone knows you don't go hill-climbing or trekking alone.

Except Pete, that is. They say you can read a person by how he drives. Add to that, how he climbs. Reckless and no thought for others, that's Pete. He's been known to disappear without a word and come back a week later to announce he's been across somewhere like Exmoor, through wind, rain, ice and whatever else. On his own. When we tell him he's a crazy idiot, he laughs as if we're the flumps.

Sometimes, I'm sure he performs these stunts only so he can laugh at us later. "The only way to improve is to keep doing it," he tells us. "If you wait for others, you'll never do anything. Get out there, you mopey load of wankers." But he's wrong. Hill-climbing and trekking are not, and never have been, solitary activities. You don't go hill-climbing in search of Zen inner peace. It's you against Nature. If you don't have someone with you, one day when you least expect it, you'll not come back. That's true for everyone, however good they think they are.

So here we are. The Brecon Beacons. According to Pete's map, we hike across some fields, through trees and undergrowth, up and down a steep rise and, finally, over craggy terrain. That's more than three miles to the foot of the first climb.

Fifteen minutes in, the car is out of sight and we're on our way, Pete leading at a good pace. Me, I'm not so fast.

After a few more minutes, I call out. "Pete."

He stops, turns and waits for me to catch up.

"Did you switch the lights off?"

"What?"

"Did you switch the lights off?"

"Yeah, course I did. What do you think I am?"

"Wanted to make sure," I say. "Can't remember seeing you do it, that's all."

We carry on for another ten minutes or so. He stops, turns and looks over my shoulder at the way we've come. Darkness has almost lifted. He looks at his watch.

"Thirty-five minutes," he says.

"What?"

"We've been going thirty-five minutes." He's studying his watch. "I could be there and back in thirty." He's taking off his backpack and dropping it to the ground.

"Where are you going?" I say.

203

"The lights, I've got to check the bastards, haven't I?"

"Pete – "

"We're stymied when we get back if I left 'em on, aren't we?" he says. "And I've gotta go all the way because you got me to park against that wall, so I can't see the lights until I'm there." He leaves me sitting on his backpack as he strides off the way we came.

He takes thirty-eight minutes. His shirt is hanging out beneath his bright orange anorak. He's red-faced and sweating. He coughs an almighty hacking cough and spits at some rocks. "I'd switched them off. I'd switched them off."

I don't get up. "Well, at least now you know everything's all right. Take a few minutes. Get your breath."

"We've lost too much time," he says, bending down and heaving on his backpack. He stretches his arms out to settle the straps and off he goes without another word. I get up, shake myself into a comfortable position and follow. It'll be a while before he remembers I'm on the same planet.

We reach the base of the mountain. It's been full daylight for quite a while. Pete stops to adjust his trekking-stick for the gradient and carries on. He's done this climb before. I take a few more seconds to do the same.

At first, as the going is soft with it being wet or treacherous, it's a case of me of going where he's planted his stick and placed his boots. I keep my head down as I search for giveaway traces of holes and footprints. I hesitate more than a few times because the ground is covered in moss.

I hit a gulley of rocks and pebbles and I've

nowhere to plant my stick. My right boot slips on a rock. I cry out.

"Plant and pull," he shouts from above. "You know the drill. Plant and pull."

"I know, I know," I shout back. "But there's nowhere to go."

"Course there is. I did it, didn't I, so there must be," he hollers.

I fumble about, find a small patch of mud. I plant my stick, pull myself up.

"See," he shouts, "you can do it." He turns away and carries on.

I stumble on in my own way, in my own time. I hit another rock pile and, plant and pull, plant and pull, clamber through it. I stop to adjust the height of my stick. Mistakenly, and I should've known better, I grab some gorse thorns but hardly notice the pain. Compared with everything else that's going on, it doesn't matter anyway. Plant and pull, plant and pull.

Then I'm at the top where Pete's standing, waiting for me, smiling. "See, you did it."

"Bloody hell," I say. "Bloody hell."

"Y'okay?"

I breathe deeply.

"That's why I chose this climb," he says. "To challenge you. So you get some new experience under your belt. By the time we've completed the day, you'll be able to say you've done something you haven't done before."

"Yeah," I say, not looking at him. "I know that already."

I pull out a bottle of water and take a long drink.

"Careful how you use that," he says. "It's a long way yet." He pulls out a map.

He folds it so we can see exactly where we are. He

runs his finger over it and looks into the far distance. "See that ridge," he says, pointing ahead. "We trek along here for four and a bit miles. Then over that ridge. After that, you'll see the target mountain. We climb that, down the other side and a slow descent to the baseline."

I stare ahead. It's quite a trek. And then the climb. It'll take all day. "How far to the car after that?"

"Once we get back to baseline, about seven miles," he says, folding the map, putting it away, hitching up his trousers, patting his backpack. And so, like before, off he goes, not another word, expecting me to be ready before I know I'm supposed to be and he's a quarter of a mile away even before I've started. He doesn't look back – not once.

We're marching across a plateau, following a narrow trail where someone has been before. It's covered with rocks, strewn with brown heather, fern and the odd hawthorn or gorse bush. A stream filters its way through the terrain, sometimes on the surface, sometimes below it. After a while, I give up trying to avoid it. I let it run over my boots. The ridge Pete pointed to earlier is clearly visible and gets bigger every five hundred paces.

Sometimes, as I go into a dip, I lose sight of him. Other times, I see him as he goes over a steep mound. And still, he doesn't look back. I stop for a pee or linger to examine a fossil or rock. I'm in no hurry. Soon, I've no idea where he is. I can't even see him. I check my mobile. No signal. Which means, of course, that Pete's got no signal, either. We're out of contact.

"There you are, you snivelling snail," he shouts about an hour later. We're still hiking across the plateau. It's getting cooler by the minute and, as we're at the base of the ridge, the air grows more and more damp. "What took you so long?"

Before I can open my mouth, he's strides over. "Take the map. I want you to orientate us."

I take the map, stare at it and look up. The terrain ahead is very steep. From where I'm standing, it's an exact vertical rise. Its massive shadow overpowers my sight and I see an enormous cloud covering its peak. To our right, there's a sheer drop down on to some merciless boulders. I try to find our location on the map.

Pete stands there, pulling at his beard. After a few minutes, he barks, "Where's north?" He undoes his trousers and pees while we're standing there. "Do I have to get my compass?"

"No," I say, in a furious sweat. "We'll use mine." I fumble about in my bag and grab it, carefully making sure nothing else spills out.

"Position your map according to directional north," he lectures. "That's north," he says, pointing with one hand while still peeing with the other.

I turn it.

He finishes, tucks it in, zips up his trousers and steps forward to look over my shoulder. "You twat," he says. "You've got the map upside-down. Hold it so it points in the same direction as compass north."

I turn it again.

"If you haven't got your map positioned correctly," he says, "you haven't got a cat in hell's chance of interpreting the situation correctly. Find north and you know where you are. If you read the map upside-down, you're finished."

After another a drink and before I know it, we're climbing the ridge. The terrain is the same – worn out heather, sharp rocks, gorse, fern, rivulets, mud. Sometimes my toes catch themselves in my woollen socks, sometimes my thighs ache, the soles of my feet hurt and my nipples chafe. My balls go in on themselves, drop, catch, shrink.

We're standing at the top of the climb, peering down at where we've come. It's turned really cool. A drizzle appears. Visibility diminishes. But I'm feeling fine, getting excited.

Pete points into the far distance to the grey shadowed outline of another mountain. "See that?" he says. "That's where we're headed. We trek to the base, a bit more than an hour, rest, eat our sandwiches, have a drink. Climb to the top. Then downhill all the way."

We reach the base of the final climb. I've eaten my raspberry jam sandwiches and am munching on a completely delicious chocolate-covered cereal bar. Pete's drunk from his water-bottle.

"You see, Mark," he says, leaning towards me, pulling on his beard, "one woman's not enough. I love Angie, course I do. She's knows I do. You know I do. But she's not, how can I put this, I need more. Know what I mean?"

"Oh sure," I say, not wanting to hear this.

He takes off his beanie and gives his head a good scratch. "I don't understand it. I mean, I keep myself in shape, I've got a great appetite, I'm always ready for it, day or night, bedroom, garden, backseat of the car, I don't care. But she's not – if it weren't for – I don't know how I'd cope."

I crush the wrapper and push it my pocket.

"I mean," he says, "you get it where you can, don't you?"

He stares at me. I hope I don't look as sick and horrified as I feel. He stands up so his crotch is at my eye-level. He grabs himself and laughs his head off like a rampaging bear. An echo hits the hills.

"Fuckety fuck fuck, Mark" he shouts at the top of his voice, "we don't all lead timid lives like you. Some of us need a bit more than once every Sunday afternoon and a wank when she's not up for it."

I stand up. "That's a bit much."

"You're right, mate, sorry," he says, calming down. "You and me, we're okay. I've always liked you." He blows his nose. "But get it while you can, that's my advice," he says, inspecting his handkerchief. "'Cos you never know when it'll be your last fuck."

We've reached the final climb. I take my time 'cos I have to keep alert. The higher we go, the colder it turns. Drizzle is full on. Pete forges ahead, thinking it's a competition. Me, I'm not interested. I want to be safe. This is a hard, tough situation. Sometimes, he turns, stands, sees me struggling and laughs his head off.

Later – not concentrating - not watching what I'm doing - I plant my stick, miss my aim and it scrapes against a boulder. It slides down. I keep a good grip on the handle, knowing it's going to go through my upper right boot. I shift to avoid it. It slips against the damp grass and I fall forward. I graze my left hand against some pebbles, scream and lay there, face down. Physically, I'm okay. The shock and humili-ation daze me.

"Hey, mate" – Pete's holding me – "take it easy, eh. Don't move. Get yourself together," he whispers gently. Crouching beside me, he's taken my stick and lain it to one side. "You'll be okay," he whispers again. "Only thing that's broken is your pride."

After a few minutes, I sit up. He's there, smiling softly, holding me, watching me. "Y' all right?" he whispers. "Can you get up?"

"Yeah. Sorry." I can feel my face flushing red.

He helps me up, hands me my stick. "Never say sorry," he says. "Happens to the best of us. You missed your footing, that's all," he says. "Best thing is, get up, get on. The more you stay like this, the more unnerved you'll be. C'm' on."

He helps me up. He stands at the top, waiting. Eventually, I'm next to him.

"Made it," he says. He holds out his hand. We shake. "We've got a bit of walking," he says, looking about. "Coupla miles, maybe. Then we descend. Cloud and mist everywhere so we need to keep close together."

"No wandering off," I say.

"No wandering off."

But before I get my breath and hitch myself up ready to go, he's off and it's only a few minutes before he's out of sight, lost in – well, Pete calls it cloud and mist. I call it fog. Thick autumn fog. And cloud. And more fog. It's very cold.

I try to keep up but soon I slow down. He's out of sight, probably paying no attention to anything except what he's doing.

I stop. I stand in the middle of the trail I think he's following. I make out some rocks to my right. Rime covers the desolate heather, moss and grass. Streamlets run around my boots. It's getting even colder by the minute.

I take off my backpack and drop it to the ground. I've got a map somewhere – I've not needed it before – we've been using Pete's. I unzip a pocket, get it out. From another pocket, I get a torch. I need my compass, which I know is handy because we used it earlier. I get it out. I feel inside a third pocket to check Pete's compass is where I stashed it while he was walking back to the car to check the lights. I knew they were off before I suggested they weren't, of course.

It's a long trek back to the cottage, as obviously I can't use Pete's car. If my planning and timing work out, I'll be there shortly after dark. As I descend the ridge, the cloud, fog and the mist gradually disperse and the temperature rises. Easy enough. After all, I did this climb on my own a couple of weeks ago. I'm not the beginner Pete thinks I am – and, anyway, he thinks everyone's a beginner compared to him.

I take my time across the fields. I stride past Pete's car as if it's not there. It's sixteen miles hiking with my backpack until I'm at the cottage. It's dark. I let myself in. I put away the washing-up so it's not clear how many people stayed there. I get some clean sheets and a pillow case from the linen cupboard and make my bed. I stuff the used ones in a plastic carrier-bag which I'll take away and dump. I step carefully over Pete's scattered clothes and the towel he threw across the kitchen. I gather up my stuff.

I lock the front door, put the key in my pocket, load up the car and drive off. I've booked a room in a Travelodge in Worcester. It's the best night's sleep I've had for a long time.

For nearly a week, I'm googling every hour for a dead body found in the Brecon Beacons. I'm jumpy at work. Nobody notices. I'm tetchy at home. Sarah doesn't notice. She's never at home, anyway, what with work, aerobics, the kids and whatever else she's up to.

Six days later, it's on the radio. As I'd planned, the alarm wasn't raised for a couple of days – I'd persuaded Pete to book the cottage for five days – not until the owner goes in to clean. She finds Pete's stuff still strewn about, comes back a few hours later and he still hasn't cleared up and gone. She doesn't know what to do, her next guests turn up while she's trying to decide. They call the police.

The Mountain Rescue Team finds a body in a bright orange anorak face down in a gulley stream. One of his legs is broken. It's Pete. The police contact his wife. They issue a statement advising hill climbers not to go out trekking without telling someone where they're going – and to make sure they take at least compass, map and distress flares.

He must've used the flares – not much use when you're lost in thick fog immersed in a raining cloud – so they say he hadn't taken any. The battery on his iPhone is dead which is why the GPS failed. They can't find his compass.

Everyone from the climbing club attends the funeral. Like the other blokes there, I'm wearing my weddings and funerals suit. His wife gets very upset. The twins are too young to understand what's happening.

"You went climbing with him, didn't you, Mark?" someone says.

"Now and then, that's all. If only I'd known – " I pretend to be too upset to carry on.

Someone puts their arm around me. "Yeah. We understand, mate. It's tough for us all."

Afterwards, the club goes to the pub. Everyone says how upset they are over Pete's death. Someone suggests an annual Peter Tarleton Memorial Climb. Someone else mutters how he'd never liked Pete. Someone else says he hadn't, either. And someone else, can't remember who, says he's never forgiven him for having it off with his wife. "Matter of fact, it's because of him we're divorced. Don't expect any tears from me."

Then we're talking about something else and telling dirty jokes and Pete is forgotten.

I get home. I've had a few so I'm a bit woozy.

Sarah's in the kitchen with a suitcase, putting on her coat.

"There you are," she says. "I wanted to be gone before you got back."

She's telling me something but I can't make out what it is, the silly bitch.

"What?" I say. "What?"

"I've found someone else."

"I get home from Pete Tarleton's funeral," I say, "and you're leaving me?"

"Keep away," she says, backing away, gripping the sink.

"What?" I gurgle. "Do you think I'm going to hit you or something?"

"If I'm not out of here in the next fifteen minutes," she says, "he's calling the police."

"Who was it?" I say, backing off, trying to keep balance. "Did I know him?"

"Was? Did?" she says. "He's not a corpse, Mark. He's very much alive, thank you very much."

"Who was, is, the lucky man?"

"Paul. From work," she says. "You've met him."

"Not Paul Trimble?" I holler, stumbling against a wall. "That fat oaf who has to walk sideways to get through a door?"

"You're drunk. Again."

"No, I'm not."

"I can't take it any more," she says. "Paul is kind. He makes me laugh… and he's always here for me." She dares – dares – to walk towards me. "Which is

213

more than you are."

"He's got a wife."

"They're getting a divorce."

"How long has this been going on?" I say, trying to stay up against the wall.

She turns to the wall calendar. "See for yourself." She points to where she's written the letters PT against every Tuesday and Friday for – I flick the pages and decipher her writing as it blurs in and out of focus - what has been the last seven months.

"PT?" I say. "You said that was your personal trainer – "

" – I didn't – "

" – at that lowlife gym you go to."

"Lowlife?"

"Where are Ian and Craig?"

"Thanks for remembering them."

"Fuck you, Sarah," I shout. "Where are my fucking kids?"

"You're not going near them, you bully." She picks up the suitcase. "I gave you every chance, Mark. You could've worked it out."

"Worked it out? Personal Trainer, Paul Trimble, Pete – "

Someone knocks at the door. The doorbell rings. The racket does my head in. I'm sliding down until I'm up against the wall, legs spread out. She picks up her case, steps over me, goes into the hall.

"That fucking lump of lard must be a fucking good fuck, that's all I can fucking say," I bawl after her.

She opens the door.

"I love you, Sarah!"

The door closes. A few minutes later, I hear a car drive off.

"Where's north?" I mutter before throwing up over my suit and falling asleep.

Lightning Source UK Ltd.
Milton Keynes UK
UKOW03f1258240417
299780UK00002B/49/P